CURTAIN CALL

Harem of Freaks Book 6

CRYSTAL ASH

I shut the door behind me as quietly as I could, then grabbed Bella's tiny hand as we descended the rickety, rotting porch steps.

"Grab Joey's hand, Bells," I told my younger sister.

"Got it," she replied, in a voice that sounded too confident for one being so young—for why we were sneaking off like thieves in the night in the first place.

"Where are we going?" Riley mumbled, still half-asleep. The youngest of my siblings, a toddler of three years old, curled up against my chest with my arm holding her securely to my hip.

"We're going on an adventure, Riley." I kissed her forehead and tucked her hair under her hood before quickly glancing in both directions. We took off out of the park and across the street. Bella and Joey kept their hands clasped and trailed after me like a row of ducklings following their mother.

I wasn't their mother. Neither was Mel. But when

raising the little ones fell on us, we had no other choice. We had to be strong and protect them.

Mel looked after me and the others until she couldn't take any more and left. Maybe she knowingly passed on that responsibility to me, then again, maybe not. Just that morning, we all woke and realized she was gone. I promised myself a long time ago that I wouldn't leave unless I took all the little ones with me.

That day came this morning.

The sun wasn't even up yet and a chill hung in the air. Later, it would feel like the end of summer again, but the coolness of the night was settling in longer throughout the day.

"Walk fast, you guys," I said in a hushed whisper, trying to keep my steps slow enough for Bella and Joey to keep up. The wild crashing of my heart felt like it would explode. I fought the urge to look over my shoulder, to look back at the hell hole we just left. Mel never looked back. I was sure of that.

"Where are we going?" The plea came from Joey this time. He had slowed to a stop and was pulling back on Bella's hand, which slowed all of us down. "I'm tired. I wanna go back to bed," he whimpered.

"Joey." I stopped and turned, dropping to his eye level. "You'll go to bed soon, buddy. But we have a new home now. We just have to walk to it first, okay? Then you can sleep in super late, I promise."

"Why are we going to a new home?" His big brown eyes, so much like Mel's, shined like amber under the streetlight.

"We're going somewhere you guys won't hear Mom yelling anymore," I told him, trying to make my voice sound excited. "You won't have to hide under your beds. You won't be scared anymore. And you'll get to see Mel again, all the time! Don't you miss her?"

"Really?" His wide-eyed gaze broke my heart. His six-year-old mind probably couldn't grasp the thought of a house without yelling and not being scared. Neither could I, until I met my boyfriend Dustin's family.

Ex-boyfriend, I reminded myself.

My first thought was to run to his house, but I couldn't burden his family with all of us. He was so sweet and kind, I hated burdening him with any of the shit I dealt with at home. As much as it killed me, I broke up with him, because he deserved better.

"Yes, Joey." I rubbed some sleep out of his eyes that still lingered. "But we have to get there first. You gotta be a brave boy and walk with me, okay?"

He nodded solemnly and took Bella's hand again. I turned to her, rubbing my thumb across her small fingers. "How are you doing, Bells? Feel good, okay to keep going?"

She bobbed her head yes, sticking her chin out proudly like she wasn't even aware of the dark bruising settling in around her eye. For the first time, something got thrown, and I wasn't fast enough to block it from hitting one of the kids. But Bella was.

"Good girl." I booped her nose and returned to standing. "Let's go, gang."

I didn't let out a breath until we left the shitty, rundown neighborhood and entered the downtown area of Waterford. The sky was just beginning to light with the dawn, and the first cars on the road for work passed by us.

Drivers rubbernecked like they never saw a teenage girl hauling along three kids before. It was a common sight around these parts, but people never tired of staring like I was a goddamn zoo animal.

Riley was getting antsy, and the other two were starting to fade when we still had a mile or so to go. I allowed us to stop and rest at a bus stop, but only for five minutes. Every minute we lingered gave *him* more time to catch up to us.

Finally, we made it to the downtown Waterford homeless shelter. I checked us in, but the regretful look on the volunteer's face filled me with dread. When she told me the situation, I knew it was time to make the call. I had to swallow my pride and ask for help.

I had to set Riley down, thanks to my arm being thoroughly numb, and gave them all snacks from my backpack while I made the phone call. I dialed the one number I had committed to memory and put the receiver to my ear.

The one she gave me when she came back, right before Mom got in her face and made her leave again.

My heartbeat started going crazy again as the phone on the other end rang and rang and rang.

MELODY

"We miss you, Mel! When are you coming back?"

"Aww, I miss you guys too!" Holding the phone out in front of me so Connor and Hunter could clearly see Roo and Rinna on the screen, I smiled back at the adorable pups. "We'll be back soon. We just need to finish some work down here."

"Well, hurry up! You're missing all my big kills! I took down a buck all by myself!" Roo declared, puffing himself up proudly.

"You did not, that was Uncle Colt and Uncle Gabe!" Rinna ratted him out, much to our amusement.

"Well, I helped!"

"Alright, guys," Hunter removed his arm from around my shoulders to take hold of the phone. "It's past your bedtime. Be good and do what your uncles tell you, or I'll drag you by your scruffs when I get back."

"We will!" they sang in unison. "Goodnight, Dad! We love you!"

"Goodnight. Love you guys too."

The warmth and love in his voice made me melt into a puddle. I placed my head on his shoulder and curled my legs underneath me, leaning on him heavily. We'd been eating dinner and catching up in our Miami hotel restaurant, but I still couldn't believe my wolf was back.

His brothers showed up out of the blue to our house in Georgia, right around the same time we got a job offer hundreds of miles away in Florida. For thirty-thousand dollars, we just couldn't say no. However, we had a strong possibility of working long-term for the Vaudeville Theater, and Hunter wasn't sure if he'd be willing to leave his family so soon after being reunited.

He had Raz and I in limbo for a few days—we didn't know whether to treat this like a breakup or some kind of long-distance relationship when Hunter showed up in Miami. He chose us. His mates.

He left his pups in the temporary care of his brothers and their shaman, Miriam. We would soon return to the Georgia house and weren't sure what the Vaudeville would offer us yet. But there was still the massive shifter compound to deal with.

On the other side of me, in the round booth table, Connor stroked my calf and leaned over to kiss my shoulder.

"I'll be back in a while, babe. Meet you guys back in the suite."

"Where are you off to?" I asked, watching him slide out the opposite side.

"You'll see," he answered evasively. "Keep her safe while I'm gone, Hunter."

"She's never been safer," Hunter replied, draping his long arm over me again.

"My knights in shining armor," I huffed, rolling my eyes.

Hunter chuckled, dropping a kiss to my head. "You just bring out the animal in all of us. In more ways than one."

"Naughty wolf," I teased, wrapping an arm around his waist. I could still feel the effects of the orgasms he and Raz had given me hours earlier. The three of us had quite the reunion when our wolf returned and told us he was staying.

Thinking of Raz made me lift my head off Hunter's chest. When we joined Connor for dinner, he and Arjun went to scope out the restaurant where they captured Julian, a young coyote shifter I was able to Speak to psychically. Over an hour had passed now, and I wondered if my dragon and the tiger were okay.

"What's up?" Hunter noticed the shift in my body.

"I was just thinking of Raz and Arjun," I told him. "I hope they haven't run into any trouble." I didn't want to voice my fear of them being captured. If they were caught, the chances of us finding the shifter compound were slim to none, not to mention getting in and freeing everyone.

"I'm sure they are." He massaged my hip soothingly. "Why don't you check in with them? Can you use Speak when they're in human form?"

"Not sure. I've never tried it."

I closed my eyes, picturing my handsome tattooed dragon in my head, and decided to try.

Hey, Raz. Can you hear me?

Steluța, he answered immediately. Yes, you're loud and clear, my love. What is it?

Just checking in. How are you guys?

He hesitated for a moment before answering.

Physically, we're fine. We've found a way into the compound and have learned some new developments. We're heading back to the hotel now and will give you a full update.

Okay, I replied. See you soon.

"They're okay and heading back," I reported to Hunter, lifting my head off him and sitting up straight.

"You don't seem all that happy," he observed, locking those golden eyes on me.

I chewed my lip, mulling over Raz's choice of words. "He said they were physically fine, implying they're *not* okay in other ways."

"Hm." Hunter pursed his lips thoughtfully. "I guess we'll find out when they get back."

"Now I'm going to worry until the moment I see they're alive and well," I muttered, sliding out of the booth and straightening my clothes. "Especially after all the mind shit I had gone through. I wouldn't wish that on anybody."

On our way down to Florida, I started having increasingly worse headaches. The pain kept growing exponentially until I saw horrific visions of what the compound shifters were going through in real time. Not only could I see through their eyes, I heard their cries and felt all of their pain in my own body. To say it was unbearable was putting it lightly.

What got me through it was Arjun, much to my surprise. He'd really saved me in so many ways while we were down here. Maybe it was my imagination, but I could swear we were getting closer. The guys insisted he liked me, but he always kept me at arm's reach. Except for the times that he didn't.

"Arjun and Raz are strong. I'm sure they're fine." Hunter rubbed my back as he followed me out of the booth and back to the hotel lobby. "Seems like the tiger's got a thing for my little fox," he teased, pulling me to his side.

"Don't start," I groaned. "I mean, I'm not opposed to the idea, but one minute Arjun's firmly against it, and the next, he's touching my hand and shit. I've talked about it with Connor and Raz and it's... complicated."

"Aw, what's throwing one more shifter into our little love triangle?" he laughed. "Or I guess we're a love square, actually. With Arjun thrown in, what does that make us? A love pentagon?"

"Stop," I giggled, poking him in the ribs. "Speaking of love triangle, I'm really happy you claimed Raz as a mate."

"Yeah?" His cheeks flushed and an adorable smile played at his lips. "I probably should have talked about that with you, since it was you and me first. But I was thinking about it the whole trip down here and it just... felt right."

"Then it is right." I wrapped an arm around his waist as we ascended the winding staircase to our suite level. Sure, we could have taken the elevator, but this gave us more time to talk. "And I have two other mates, for Christ's sake. You don't need my permission to have one more."

"Still, I don't ever want you to feel disrespected again."

His fingers squeezed around my shoulder. He was referring to his brother Gabe, shooting me a dirty look back home. It wasn't a huge deal to me, but my guys seemed to take it as a major offense. At that point, I fully understood why shifters held such a deep hatred for humans. Though Connor and Raz were ready to chase some wolves back into the woods.

I looked up at Hunter, smiling broadly. We were all new to this multi-person relationship and still figuring out our way around it. He wanted to keep me aware of his intentions and I appreciated that, but the way he claimed Raz and me was just perfect.

"You know, I don't think Raz has felt loved by anyone before this," I said. "I mean, he knows he's sexy and charming. His adult life has always been about surviving and occasionally having meaningless sex."

"Now he has two people that love him," Hunter agreed softly.

"Yeah," I answered. "Being someone's mate. I think it means a lot to him."

We reached the suite to find Connor waiting for us, a small plastic grocery bag in his hand.

"Gonna tell us where you ran off to, now?" I asked, eyeing the bag.

"Babe, you can see plain as day where I ran off to," he remarked, holding up the bag. "The question is what did I get?" He shook it at me tauntingly.

"Don't keep me in suspense now." I rolled my eyes, crossing my arms. "Did you get me a Walmart engagement ring?"

"Please, we just made like forty-grand in a single night! The rock I get you is going to be worth at *least* that much."

"I'm telling you right now, don't waste our money," I laughed with a shake of my head. "But really, what did you get?"

He shot a sneaky glance toward Hunter before reaching into the bag and holding its contents out in his hand. My heart leaped into my throat when I saw what laid across his palm.

"Pregnancy tests?!"

"Yeah, I got a bunch of different ones." He shook the bag in his opposite hand.

"Connor, uh..." Why did my face feel so hot? Why was I suddenly so fucking nervous? "I think it's too soon to tell. My period isn't due for a while so I'm not sure if I'm going to miss it."

"I remember you saying that, so I got some early detection ones too." He rummaged through the bag and pulled out one to read it. "Yep, here we go! As early as a week after conception, it says." He held it out to me, his forest green eyes lit up like a Christmas tree. "Babe, don't you want to know?"

"Of course I do," I told him. "I just think we're jumping the gun a little."

"She knows her body best, Con," Hunter added.

"Well, try this early one and if it's negative, we'll try again when your period is due. And if the red tide rolls in, I guess that'll be our answer."

That sounded like a reasonable request. I just couldn't figure out why it felt like he was asking me to jump out of a plane.

I took the box from him with slow, hesitant hands. I turned it over to read the directions, but the small writing just blurred together.

"I love you, babe." Connor pulled me close and kissed my temple. "No matter what the results are. We're all here for you."

While I didn't know whether to be excited or scared to death, Connor was an electric ball of excitement. He was trying to be calm and strong, but I saw the hope in his eyes. He wanted me to be pregnant, to grow big and round with a product of our love. And I wanted to give that to him, more than anything.

I wanted to give him a baby so badly, I didn't know if I could handle the disappointment of a negative test. Sure, we could try again later. Still, so many aspects of our lives were up in the air—the compound shifters, my siblings, finding a forever home and being able to afford one for our big, mixed-species family.

All of these thoughts jumbled through my head as I marched like a zombie to the bathroom. My hands pulled down my shorts and underwear as I sat on the toilet mechanically.

A random statistic popped into my head, as they often did when my thoughts wandered all over the place. Something like a third of all pregnancies don't ever fully develop. Many women miscarry before they even realized they were pregnant.

It hit me just as I started to open the packaging on the test. My hands froze as my mind became clear. Then, just as quickly as I sat down, I stood up and pulled my clothes back on.

When I returned to the living room, Connor crossed his arms and arched a skeptical brow at me.

"Now I know you women are speedy about this shit, but you did *not* just take a leak, babe."

"I'm sorry," I told him, placing the unopened pregnancy test back in the bag. "But I can't do this. Not right now."

2

MELODY

A look of hurt crossed Connor's face before he put on a mask of neutrality. "Why not?" He posed the question casually.

"Because if I take that test and find out that I *am* pregnant," I swallowed. "You guys would do everything in your power to protect me and keep me, *us*, out of danger."

"Naturally." Connor narrowed his eyes, now confused. "Of course we would, babe. Why's that an issue?"

"It's not, not normally," I answered. "But we have to take risks in order to save the shifters at the compound. We're all going to risk our lives, most likely. If something happens to me—"

"Babe!"

"If something happened to me or the baby," my hand drifted over my stomach. "I'd rather not know I was carrying. Not this early. With everything else going on, I couldn't live with knowing I lost—"

"Shhh." Hunter pulled my head onto his chest, his

hands soothing over my back and in my hair. "I get it, little fox. I understand."

"You do?" I looked up at him, resting my chin on his chest.

He nodded, looking sad. "Roo and Rinna were not our first attempts at conceiving. My former mate lost our first pups early in her pregnancy, but it was no less devastating. We almost wish we hadn't known."

That floored me. I had no idea Hunter dealt with such a loss. He lost his pups, his mate, his entire pack, and had been captured. And while he wasn't perfect, my pale wolf was still an amazing mate and father. He could have let the events of his life destroy him, but he didn't.

"We're protecting you regardless if you're pregnant or not," Connor said. "No one is letting you get hurt by those sick fucks."

"All I'm saying is, there's going to be risks we can't predict," I told him, now wishing I had Miriam's ability to see a glimpse into the future. "If we find out I'm pregnant, y'all probably won't let me leave the suite and that's a no-go from me. I won't let you guys risk your lives while I'm locked away in an ivory tower."

Connor rubbed his jaw, a grin threatening to emerge on his lips. "I have half a mind to tie you to the bed, anyway."

"I'd be in favor of that," Hunter agreed.

"I know you guys are joking," I sighed, "but seriously, this is my decision. I'll take the test after everything is done. I don't want to be treated differently, and I don't want to grieve a loss if something were to happen. Maybe that's selfish, but it's how I feel."

"Of course it's your decision, babe." Connor's serious face returned. "I'm bummed because I was dying to find out, but it's totally up to you. However you feel is more important."

"Thank you," I told him, feeling several pounds lighter. I approached him and unfolded his arms to put them around me, where they belonged.

Just then we heard the sound of a keycard sliding through the electronic lock on the door.

"They're back!" I breathed, spinning in his arms to watch eagerly for Raz and Arjun to come through the door. The moment they did, it was like all the air got sucked out of the room.

Arjun headed straight for his room, not even making eye contact with anyone, before slamming his door shut. The sound reverberated throughout the suite like he had used all his strength. We all turned to Raz with silence and wide eyes for an explanation.

With a sigh, he leaned his back against the front door and looked toward the ceiling, displaying his sexy throat tattoos. "Shit is fucked," was all he said.

"What happened?" Hunter asked. He reached forward and took a light hold on Raz's hand, gently pulling our dragon toward us.

"Are you okay?" I grabbed his other arm as he came forward, looking for my answer in those steel-gray eyes.

"I'm fine, *steluța*," he gave me a reassuring smile before lifting his eyes toward Arjun's room. "He's not."

"Why?" A rush of emotions overcame me. If it weren't for Connor wrapped around me, I might have marched over to Arjun's door to check on him. If he wasn't okay, he shouldn't be alone. He'd basically saved my life on this trip. The least I could do was be there for him, too.

"Let's all sit down," Connor suggested.

Hunter and I sandwiched Raz between us on the couch while Connor took the oversized armchair to himself.

"We went to La Hacienda," Raz began. "Arjun spotted a guy right away, heading toward the back room where Julian was taken. He said he smelled like blood and tranquilizers, and he could also faintly smell other shifters who had been back there before."

"Oh God," I whispered, my stomach churning. How many had been baited to go back there just like Julian?

"The door at the end of the hall was locked, but we followed the trail outside and behind the restaurant. Arj stayed on his scent trail, and I could feel the guy's footsteps," Raz continued. "We followed for a few blocks and then it was gone. The scent dead-ended and I couldn't feel any vibrations of movement in the air. It was like he disappeared, or turned into a statue and covered up his trail."

"How is that possible?" Connor wondered aloud.

"Shaman illusions," I answered. I couldn't explain how I knew, but it somehow made sense to me. It was a simple game of opposites. Cover up movement and you have stillness. Cover up the scent and you remove the trail.

"Yes, exactly," Raz looked at me. "But this was nothing like what I've seen you do. Arjun picked up a rock and threw it above our heads. It bounced off something that sounded like a metal door, even though we couldn't see anything there."

"Whoa," Hunter leaned back in his seat. "So this place is really hiding in plain sight. This shaman can cast an illusion to hide an entire compound?"

"Yes, and apparently there's only one who can do that," Raz sighed. "Arjun deduced it must be his stepfather, Lhozen."

"*What?*" the three of us demanded in unison.

"Isn't this the guy who raised him?" Connor asked.

"He was married to a shifter, Arjun's mom! How could he do this?" I demanded.

"He taught Miriam everything she knows, and she wouldn't hurt a fly," Hunter voiced. "I trust her as much as my brothers, which was the only reason I left my kids with them."

"I asked him a lot of the same questions," Raz answered sadly. "He's convinced that he's right, but naturally, he's all torn up about it now. He was silent and brooding the entire way back, like he just tuned me out. I think he needs to be alone for now."

"Damn." I leaned back on the couch, mirroring Hunter. "Poor Arjun. What a terrible thing to find out."

"Jesus tap-dancing Christ," Connor groaned, rubbing a hand down his face. "So what the hell are we dealing with here?"

"Someone who knows both shifters and humans very intimately, and is powerful enough to fool them both," Raz muttered. "A goddamn fucking magician."

"Something tells me that doesn't make our chances any better," Connor replied.

"I'm really going to need Arjun's help," I realized, folding my hands in my lap. "He knows Lhozen better than anyone. If anyone knows how to see through his illusions, it's him. He proved that already with the rock and the invisible door."

"Sure, but how much will he want to help?" Hunter asked. "I'm not sure how close he and Lhozen were, but this must be a monumental betrayal to him. It's his father... stepfather. Is he going to have his head in the game? We have to beat him—Maybe even kill him?"

The room was silent for a moment, all of us deep in our own heads as we pondered those questions. But nobody could answer them, except for the tiger shifter locked away in his room.

❧ 3 ❧

MELODY

We decided to leave Arjun alone for the night, and try gauging his feelings in the morning. As the four of us got ready for bed, the space issues in our love square became clear.

"How the fuck are we all gonna fit?" Connor demanded, looking between all of us and the king-sized bed. "I'll tell y'all right now, I'm not cuddling with anyone besides Mel."

"It'll be a bit of a squeeze, but the wolf and I can snuggle up close." Raz kissed Hunter's neck before peeling his shirt off. "You should have plenty of room to spread out like a starfish, Con, on your side of the bed."

"I do not spread out like a starfish. I sleep like the dead. That's the only reason you got away with it that one time ... fucking our girl right next to me, you sneaky bastard."

"You told him about that?!" Raz demanded, his mouth hanging open in mock betrayal.

"He had me pressed against a wall!" I shot back defensively. "I didn't mean to, but he'd just gotten his new legs and I couldn't think straight."

"Wow, when did I miss this?" Hunter chuckled. Now shirtless himself, he came up behind Raz to wrap his arms around the dragon's tattooed shoulders. Pulling him close, he dropped kisses to Raz's neck and shoulder, making the dragon visibly shiver at the contact and heat pool between my legs.

"When you were off with your douchebag brothers," Raz murmured in reply, leaning his head back to kiss Hunter's ear and jaw.

"What are you staring at, babe?"

Connor came up behind me, his firm hands gliding along my waist made me jump. I didn't realize how entranced I was watching the shifters being sweet to each other. It almost felt perverse, getting so turned on by them just expressing their love and affection.

"*Steluţa*, you must know by now that we love putting on a show for you," Raz grinned. "We are performers, after all." His breath hitched as Hunter turned it up even more, caressing sensually over the dragon's chest and abs. His kisses became more passionate, slow and open-mouthed, with a hint of teeth.

"Did your little reunion still leave you wanting more?" Connor's stubble was rough on my cheek and neck, his lips just grazing over my tender skin. "Is our woman just that insatiable?"

"Not that it wasn't good, but I would have liked..." Connor's mouth found my earlobe, making all words escape my breath as I arched against him, the intense sensation too good to ignore. He immediately pulled my hips back, limiting my movement and letting his bulge nestle against my ass.

"What would you have liked, little fox?" Hunter and Raz sat together on the edge of the bed, Hunter's chin resting on Raz's shoulder as his hands now massaged down the dragon's thighs. "Tell us." Raz leaned back against him, much like how I was with Connor, lifting his hips off of the bed so his jeans began sliding down from the wolf's touch.

My pulse thrummed in my veins, hotter by the second and moving fast. We hadn't even done anything yet. It was the teasing, the anticipation of watching what played out between the shifters that turned me into an instant puddle of sex-goo.

"I would have liked your cock, Hunter." The words sounded so dirty, yet empowering, coming from my mouth. "Inside me."

"Boys, did you deprive our woman of cock?" Connor held up a finger and wagged it disapprovingly. "That is *not* how you keep her satisfied. Shame on you."

"I was hoping you'd say that," Hunter grinned wolfishly over Raz's shoulder. "Because that was exactly what I wanted to give you. What happened earlier was just a warmup."

"Oh, she's warmed up alright." Connor ran his hands from my waist up over my breasts, my nipples practically stabbing his palms through my bra and top. "She barely needs any foreplay, just watching you guys."

"Come here, *steluţa*," Raz ordered, his voice low and husky. "Let me make sure you're properly warmed up."

My legs already like jello, I walked over to him, with Connor following close behind. Before straddling his legs,

I helped Hunter pull his jeans the rest of the way down. Our wolf kept kissing and teasing him, his hands playing along the waistband of his snug boxer briefs. Raz's thick head poking out of the top and his hot grunts and groans told me all about how warmed up *he* was getting.

Together, Connor and Raz helped me out of my clothes, and the feel of two pairs of hands on me was almost too much to bear. Raz's tongue made a burning trail from my lips to my nipples, the two sides flicking the stiff peaks into aching buds. Connor's mouth sent shivers along my spine, his hands and face rough on my back. It contrasted with Raz's smooth jaw and the delightfulness of his split tongue on my most sensitive areas.

I felt the bed depress behind me as Connor sat down. His chest and abs, a strong impenetrable wall, pressed against my back. Always shielding me, my protector. I turned to kiss him over my shoulder, sighing into his mouth at the feel of Raz's lips and tongue caressing my exposed neck and throat.

All four of us leaned to the side until our bodies hit the mattress. Connor and I never once broke our kiss, his firm grip holding the curve of my waist as he spooned me from behind. His cock, hot and rock hard, pressed between my ass cheeks.

In front of me, Raz and Hunter must have switched places. As I kissed Connor, soft wolfish growls vibrated along the skin of my chest. Sharp teeth closed around one of my nipples, making me gasp with a soft moan.

"Hello, little fox," Hunter murmured, his mouth traveling from one breast to the other.

"Hello, my handsome wolf," I breathed, running my

fingers through his gorgeous platinum hair while I waited for his lips to return to mine.

When his lips captured mine in a savage kiss, my hands often met with Razvan's as we both explored our wolf's body. Raz nibbled at his neck and shoulders, eliciting more soft growls from Hunter. While Hunter also gave light, teasing bites to my lips. My fingertips skimmed down his long torso to wrap around that iron hard shaft pressed between us.

He groaned at the contact and surged his hips forward, pressing hard against my clit, which made my own hips buck in response. Behind me, Connor slid his mouth along my shoulder as he pressed two fingers between my legs.

"Oh my God," he moaned into my neck, dipping those fingers into me and stroking my inner walls. "You are so ready for him, babe."

"I've been ready," I answered, my voice a low, lusty whisper. I couldn't take my eyes off Hunter's face. His golden eyes were hooded and his mouth hung open in soft, sexy pants as I stroked him from base to tip.

He looked away from me for a moment, glancing over his shoulder at Raz, who fiddled with a small bottle of lube. Raz kissed him and murmured something that sounded like, "Relax, wolf. I won't hurt you."

Taking hold of his chin, I turned Hunter back to face me, kissing him with all my pent-up need and frustration at their teasing.

"I need you," I murmured against his lips, my lower body thrashing against Connor's fingers, still pumping in and out of me.

Hunter grabbed my hips to line himself up with me and Connor's fingers withdrew, leaving me achingly empty.

My wolf pressed into me slowly, letting me savor every delectable inch of him. I seemed to forget how to breathe, like he pushed all the air out of me.

Hunter seemed to lose his breath too, but not because of being inside me. Behind him, Raz kissed him and murmured in his ear. I couldn't see everything, but the dragon's hands seemed busy near Hunter's ass.

His expression shifted from being blissed out with pleasure to mildly uncomfortable. I pressed my hands to his face, knowing he was adjusting to the new sensations Raz was giving him.

"We love you, Hunter," I whispered against his mouth. "All we want is for you to feel good."

A shudder and a hot moan escaped him before he started thrusting against me. Connor held me in place, keeping me sandwiched between them so I could only absorb the impact of Hunter's body on mine.

"That's it," Raz rasped against his ear. "Just let go. Let yourself enjoy it." His tattooed arm flexed as he played with Hunter's ass a bit more vigorously, applying more lube as needed with his other hand.

"Fuck," Hunter choked out, fucking me more erratically as his control began to slip. "Why is that so fucking good?"

"It's a little-known pleasure center for a man," Raz grinned, his eyes dark with lust as he watched our wolf's pleasure build and his control unravel.

Without warning, Hunter suddenly pulled out of me. He sucked in deep, ragged breaths. His cock jutted out, wet and glistening and flexing with more tension than a tripwire.

"I need a breather," he gasped, shooting me a sheepish grin. "Or I'll be done too fast."

"Mind if I take over, babe?" Connor was already rubbing his head over my slick, sensitive entrance.

My moans and whimpers were all the permission he needed. He pressed inside me, filling the emptiness that Hunter left behind. Still spooning me from behind, he lifted my leg for easier access to my clit while he fucked me with abandon.

"Watch them, babe," he whispered in my ear like a devil on my shoulder. "Watch your mates please each other and I dare you not to come."

Hunter and Raz made out passionately—all teeth, tongues, and rough manhandling by two alpha males. Hunter jerked Raz's thick cock, which was already slick with lube. His own cock still jutted out hard and straight as a steel rod. I could now clearly see Raz's well-lubed fingers sliding in and out of Hunter, giving our wolf pleasure that he'd never known before.

"Connor," I panted, not knowing what I was pleading for. He pinched one of my nipples, making me buck even harder against his other hand pressed firmly to my clit. My orgasm was building up so fast, I felt like I was drowning. I couldn't catch a breath, I was chasing pleasure so hard and climbing a mountain so fast.

Just when I was about to crest that peak, he released me. His cock slid out of me, feeling like a hot iron against my thigh.

"Ready to go again, Hunter?" he asked.

"Ugh, I hate you." My teeth nearly chattered, I was such a frayed bundle of nerves. He merely shot a shit-eating grin at my glare.

"I think so." Hunter rolled on his side toward me again, with Raz settling behind him. This time, I saw Raz nudge his cock toward Hunter's ass.

I scooted forward and practically impaled myself on Hunter. Call me greedy, but I wanted to see his pleasure up close and make it my own. With my hands cradling his neck, I kissed him hard. I raised and lowered myself, taking my fill of him and chasing that pleasure again.

I kept my eyes open, watching his gorgeous face in fascination as Raz slowly eased himself inside of him.

"Fuck," he gasped, abruptly cutting off our kiss. "Fuck, you're big, Raz."

"Thanks," the dragon chuckled, nuzzling his neck. "That's why I'm going slow. Just tell me if you want me to stop."

"No, it's good." Hunter's eyes fluttered in pleasure, his lips pulling back into a lopsided smile. "Enjoying this, little fox?"

"Immensely," I said. "I'm so close and it's mainly because of you two."

"Oh?" He looked over my shoulder at Connor, who propped himself up on his elbow as he gently stroked himself. "Did someone deny you an orgasm over there?"

"Yes." I shot another glare back at my Marine, who just laughed.

"I'm just teaching you to appreciate delayed gratification, babe," he returned. "Like I could have blown my load already but it's going to be so much better when I'm back inside you."

Before I could reply, Hunter let out one of the hottest moans I ever heard from him right against my throat. Raz's fingers dug into his hips, his teeth buried in his shoulder, and his cock seated all the way inside our wolf.

When Raz thrust gently, he pushed Hunter forward to thrust into me.

"Oh God," Hunter choked out, wrapping around me tightly until I was crushed to his chest. He was delirious with pleasure, and Raz and I exchanged a glance that shared how much we loved it.

While they were rougher with each other, Raz was just as sweet and attentive to Hunter as he always was to me. He kissed him and kept checking in to make sure he was feeling good. He applied a liberal amount of lube and carefully watched our wolf for any signs of discomfort. My heart wanted to burst with how much I loved them both, with how much love and care they showed each other.

Hunter looked over his shoulder to kiss Raz hungrily, wrapping an arm around the back of our dragon's head to pull him even closer. As Raz's thrusts grew deeper and more intense, so did Hunter's.

I'd been teetering on the edge for so long, I was amazed they didn't set me off instantly. Raz controlled the movement and the power, pushing Hunter into me and making my pleasure climb high with a slow, steady build.

Time seemed to slow down around us. Every look, every kiss, every thrust carried meaning. I was drowning again, but every beat of pleasure was longer, dragged out like the most luxurious morning stretch.

Every nerve in my body crackling with pent-up energy, my pleasure crested again just as Raz broke a kiss with Hunter. Their foreheads pressed against each other as each of their beautiful eyes locked.

"God, I fucking love you," Raz choked out first.

And that's when I crashed, convulsing so uncontrollably that tears came to my eyes. I didn't know if Hunter said it back. I couldn't hear anything over my blood pounding loudly in my ears. His warmth spilled inside me within seconds, his face buried in my neck, his cock still pounding into me as Raz pounded him.

His orgasm, longer and more intense than anything he had ever felt, seemed to feed my own. Our pleasure rode on each other for what had to be several minutes until the world stilled around us.

"Well, goddamn." Connor's arms came around me to gently tug me from Hunter's tight embrace. "That might have been the hottest thing I've ever seen."

I shivered at my Marine's touch, full-on body tremors from how sensitive I still was. Hunter did the same as Raz caressed him.

"Look at these two, Raz," Connor quipped. "I think you literally fucked their brains out."

"Mm. Still in there, wolf?" Raz teased Hunter, staring at the wolf adoringly. He was still hard and now nestled against the cleft of Hunter's ass.

"I just... fucking wow," Hunter panted, slapping Raz's hand over his heart. "I had no idea I could come like that."

"See what you've been missing all this time?" Raz grinned, dragging his fingertips across Hunter's pale skin to elicit even more shivers.

Returning the grin, Hunter rolled onto his back and grabbed Raz's arms, pulling him roughly on top and wrapping him in a bear hug.

"Now it's your turn," he whispered before crashing his mouth to his in a savage kiss.

"Mm, you want more of me, do ya?" Raz scooted into

position so that his cock lined up with Hunter again. Running one hand down the wolf's taut body, he sat back on his heels and applied fresh lube as he stroked himself.

"Always." Hunter licked his lips as he watched.

I playfully smacked Connor, who almost looked more transfixed by their show than I was. "Hear that? Your turn now."

"Mm-hm, you caught me," he chuckled, giving me a kiss. "Get on your knees, babe. I have a feeling you want a front-row seat to this."

He stood from the bed and I took a moment just to look at and appreciate him. A solid wall of muscle, pure strength and masculinity. His cock jutted out from that strong body like a weapon, surrounded by those powerful thighs like tree trunks. His prosthetic legs put him at the perfect height to fuck me from behind while standing.

I scooted on my knees to the edge of the bed, closing my eyes for a moment just to enjoy his hands on my hips and waist. His round head kissing my slick, sensitive entrance, but not penetrating yet.

A deep groan made my eyes open. Raz was buried deep in Hunter again, but this time, the sight of them made me want to look away. Not because it wasn't hot, it definitely was. They wrapped around each other in an intimate embrace, kissing and staring at each other, chest to chest. Anyone could tell the world melted away, and they were aware of nothing except each other. They were making love, and this was their moment.

I flipped over, staring up at my handsome Marine. He was my first love and the future father of my children, as he gave me a quizzical look.

"Come here." I crooked a finger at him with a smile. "I just want to see you and feel you right now."

I felt his smile through his kiss as he lowered to his knees and lined up with me at the edge of the bed.

"Damn, I didn't know I could love someone so much," he said in an awed whisper.

"Me neither." I locked my ankles behind his back and wrapped my arms around his neck. "Or so many people."

"I always knew your heart was too big for just me," he groaned as he pushed inside, filling me to the brim.

"But I still love you completely," I whispered, arching and leaning my head back at the wonderful fullness. "I love all of you, with all of me."

He surged in and out of me with a deep intentional rhythm. Soon the world melted away for me too, until there was nothing but his incredible body and those forest green eyes.

❧ 4 ❧

MELODY

I woke up early the next morning with an overwhelming urge to check on Arjun. The only question was how I'd get up without waking anyone else.

The eyes that stared back at me belonged to the black dragon on Raz's back. For once, he ended up as the little spoon. He and Hunter were tangled up in a mass of arms and legs like they would never separate. Connor wrapped tightly around me from behind and I struggled to get loose from his ever protective hold.

The room was still dark. It couldn't have been past five in the morning. But I slept like the dead and now felt wide awake.

After carefully extracting myself from the cuddle pile, I dressed myself in clothes that had been taken off the night before.

Hey, now that we have money, maybe I can afford some nicer clothes, I thought. *From Target or a mall, maybe.*

I walked out to the silent living room, taking a

moment to stare at the ocean in the distance. Florida really was beautiful. I found it hard to believe this tropical paradise was only two states away from the shithole where I grew up. The two places might as well had been different universes.

I wouldn't mind settling here, but only if all the guys agreed. And once we got rid of that awful shifter compound hidden right under our noses.

Before approaching Arjun's room, I went to the kitchen to prepare him a cup of tea. However moody he was feeling, tea always seemed to cheer him up. Such an Englishman thing. And if I was truly honest with myself, my heart went pitter-patter at the thought of seeing his handsome face light up. I wanted to make him happy.

I opened a tea bag and plopped in a cup of water from the tap. Then stuck it in the microwave and turned to look at the ocean again while I waited.

It was too quiet now. Too much of a... *not* home. I missed the rambunctious pups and the forest surrounding our house in Georgia. My heart ached at the thought of everyone living under the same roof again. Even having Colt and Gabe around didn't immediately fill me with dread. They seemed to have warmed up to me before we left, so we could hopefully be close neighbors. I was eager to talk to Miriam some more. Had her other Sight changed since she caught a glimpse of my future?

The microwave beeped, and I carefully removed the mug, holding it by the handle as my bare feet padded across the cool tile floor to Arjun's room. I pressed my ear to the door. Total silence.

I knocked softly. "Arjun? It's Mel."

Nothing answered from the other side, so I grabbed

the doorknob to find it was unlocked. I waited five more seconds before turning the knob and pushing the door open.

"Arjun?" I poked my head in. "I brought you tea."

He sat on the bed with his back against the headboard, still fully dressed in his clothes from yesterday. With his legs stretched out in front of him, he stared at nothing. The room was dark except for his bedside lamp. His TV was off. It was like he'd been sitting there, staring into empty space all night.

"Arjun?" I placed the cup down on the nightstand and moved closer. He didn't even react to my presence until I touched his shoulder.

"I don't understand it," he whispered. "I've been trying to connect the dots, but they simply aren't there."

"Arjun..." I didn't know what to say. His face was blank, but I felt the emotional anguish coming off him in waves. He looked up to this man, Lhozen. He trusted him and saw him as a father figure. Only to find out that same man profited from treating others—like him—like cattle.

I didn't know how to help him make sense of it, or to ease the feeling of loss and betrayal, so I just asked him, "Can I sit with you?"

He didn't answer, so I invited myself on the bed next to him, climbing up and taking the same position as him, back against the headboard and legs stretched out. When I reached for his hand, his fingers gently curling around mine were the only indication he knew I was there.

"I'm so sorry, Arjun," I told him, feeling like I was speaking to an empty room. "It's selfish of me, but all I can think about was how horrible my mother was. She never should have had kids. That was clear from the start. The best thing she could do for us was to be an example of how not to live our lives. How to not treat other people."

He didn't respond, but his thumb moved back and forth across the inside of my palm.

"But I was lucky in a way," I continued. That got a small huff of breath from him, like a scoff, so I kept going. "Since the day I was born, I knew what to expect. I knew exactly who and what she was, so I never felt disappointed and betrayed by her. She wasn't a mother, so I didn't hold her to any standards or expectations. I always knew she was just someone I had to avoid. I had to stay out of her way until I turned eighteen and I could be free."

I looked at him, all light and spark gone from those gorgeous ocean-colored eyes. I didn't even know Lhozen, but I hated him in that moment. Not even for all the shifters who suffered, but just for hurting this man sitting next to me.

"I can't even imagine how it must feel, to have someone tell you they love you, to be an actual parent who guides and protects you, and then rip that all away." I leaned my head to the side until it touched his shoulder. "Lhozen is even worse than my mother because of that. I'm so sorry that he did this to you."

He let out a long sigh, the first true sign of life since I came into the room.

"I never suffered like you," he said softly. "I never wanted for anything growing up. We weren't wealthy and mum was pretty old-school about a lot of things, but my childhood was happy. For that, I'm grateful. I can't hate him for giving us a good life when I was young. It wasn't until she died that everything got all fucked up."

His hand tightened around mine, and I felt the gentle pressure of his temple resting against my head.

"Hindus believe in reincarnation," he went on. "That the deeds of your current life determine how you will be reborn in your next life. If mum were here, she'd tell me to do nothing. That he'll answer for the suffering he's caused in his next life."

"But you don't want to do that," I speculated, and felt his confirming nod against my head.

"I want to watch him die a long, suffering death," he muttered in a low, predatory growl. "I want to taste his blood and let every shifter he's captured get a taste as well. But," he paused, "wanting such things and doing them will not bode well for my own rebirth into the next life."

"Why's that?"

"The concept of *ahimsa* is very important to Hindus," he explained. "It means do no harm, not only in actions but also in thought. Although it's moot for me. My next life is probably already determined because of all the harm I have done. It's just hard to let go of that guilt." He chuckled. "You didn't expect to come in here and listen to me ramble about my religion, did you?"

"Doesn't it make a difference if you're only harming those who've harmed you?" I asked, lifting my head off his shoulder to look at him. "You were tortured, Arjun. For years. And now you've learned this man who raised you is part of that, and torturing others. Suffering in their next life isn't enough. That ringmaster you killed deserved it. And Lhozen deserves to feel the pain he's inflicted on others in this life."

"You would make a terrible Hindu," he muttered.

"Thanks."

We both chuckled at that and he closed his other hand around mine, fingertips gently caressing the skin of my wrists and palms. It made me want to purr and curl up in his lap.

"I used to be afraid of you," I admitted, watching his hands envelop mine. "I felt every ounce of your anger and desire to kill, like it was my own. But now I know it was only aimed at those who caged you. It must be hard balancing your tiger's instincts with your peaceful beliefs."

His eyes searched mine, eyebrows lifting slightly in surprise. "Yes, it's been a lifelong struggle," he admitted. "We're told to do no harm, but we must kill for food. I spent four years in a cage and I'm supposed to just pray to Shiva. I learn my stepfather is a monster and I'm expected to let his next life be punishment enough."

"I don't know what's going to happen in your next life, or if there even is one," I said. "But you're nothing like him, Arjun. You've never harmed anyone who didn't deserve it. You deserve happiness and peace after everything you've been through."

He gave me a long, lingering look. "Why did you come in here, Mel?"

"I just wanted to check on you." Suddenly remembering, I pulled my hand from his. "And look, I brought you tea."

"So you did. Thank you, dove." He smiled for the first time, accepting the warm mug from me and taking a sip. Immediately after swallowing, he made a face. "How did you prepare this?"

"Just water and the tea bag," I answered, puzzled at his expression.

"How did you heat up the water?"

"In the microwave."

"The microwave?!"

"Well, how else am I supposed to heat it up?!"

"In a damn kettle, like a civilized human being, you muppet. And where's the milk and sugar?"

I tried to hold back my laughter, but it came spilling out as soon as he called me that name. Here we were, depressed and upset about something serious, and he was giving me shit about the tea I brought him.

"It's not funny, Mel." He tried to a keep a straight face, but the smile was breaking through, the brightness returning to his eyes. "We take our tea very seriously in England."

"I know, but..." My shoulders shook with the giggles and tears threatened to spill out of my eyes.

"I appreciate the gesture, dove, but you've fucked it up royally," he continued in a deadpan voice. "Let me show you how to make a proper cup before you attempt something like this again."

"Okay..." For some reason, the way he talked about it made it even funnier and fresh peals of laughter burst from my throat. I guess I finally got his English sense of humor.

"Come on now." He set the mug down, his grin wide and beautiful as he wrapped his arms around me. "What have you done, you silly woman?"

I didn't understand his question, so I looked up at him, my gaze captured in those eyes as deep and clear as the ocean.

Slowly, his arm dropped from around my shoulders, fingertips trailing down my back until he reached my waist. His large hand nestled in the curve there, pulling me closer. Not that he needed to. I was already close enough to see the iridescent flecks of color in his eyes, to feel the soft warmth of his breath fan across my lips.

We leaned in as if pulled magnetically toward each other. His dark lashes flickered downward, obscuring those eyes as he gazed at my lips. My hand found itself drifting up to graze across his cheek. He leaned into the touch, a catlike gesture of affection that was so uniquely him.

I tilted my head in the opposite direction, my own eyes fluttering closed as my mouth parted. His lips looked so soft and I could nearly taste their warmth as they hovered over mine.

Bang, bang, bang! "*Steluța, you in there?*"

I jumped away, startled, nearly flying out of my own skin as Raz burst into the room. He was dressed only in his boxer briefs haphazardly, like he pulled them on in a hurry and ran over here. His face looked concerned, but not at me or Arjun.

He held out Connor's phone, the screen lit up and indicating it was in the middle of a phone call. "It's your sister. She needs you."

5

MELODY

"Hello?"

"Mel?" Jeanie May's voice sounded small and far away.

"Yeah, it's me." I stood from the bed and headed for the living room, the thrill of the near-kiss with Arjun still pounding through my veins. "Where are you, Jean? Are you okay?"

"We're okay. We're at the downtown Waterford shelter." Her voice carried over calmly through the speaker, but I heard the underlying fear she swallowed down to put on a brave face for the kids.

"We?" I repeated. "Is everyone with you?"

"Yeah, we're all here. We're safe for now but we can't stay here forever." A small voice filtered through the background that sounded like Bella. "Yes, I'm talking to Mel, Bells. You can say hi in a minute."

"Jean, what happened?" I demanded, my pulse and mind racing. There were closer places to get away from the house if shit went down. If they were at the downtown shelter, it meant they walked over five miles and had zero intention of going back. They were hiding.

"It started off like any other night," she muttered. I knew she was keeping her voice low to prevent the kids from overhearing. "Mom's latest went ape-shit and started throwing glass bottles at the wall, right above Riley's crib."

"Oh no," I covered my face with my hands, the image burned behind my eyes. "Is she okay?"

"She's fine, nothing hit her," Jeanie answered. "But I was in the back bedroom helping Joey with homework. By the time I got out there, he ran out of bottles and was looking for any random shit to throw."

She paused and I heard ruffling and scratching through the phone like she was covering the mouthpiece.

"Bella was out there," she whispered. "He threw a shoe and aimed low. It got her in the face because she climbed into Riley's crib to protect her."

"Oh my God..."

"I'm okay, Mella!" Bella piped up in the background. She liked making our names sound similar, so she called us Mella and Bella. "Riley was scared and crying but I protected her."

"Yes, you did, Bells," I choked out. Someone came up behind me and rubbed my shoulders as they kissed my head, but all I could think about were my helpless baby sisters. "You're such a brave girl. But that's never going to happen again."

Jeanie repeated the message to Bella and resumed talking to me normally on the phone. "This place is crowded as shit, Mel. They don't have enough beds and our time is limited, but there's no fucking way we can go back."

"I know, Jean. I know." I rubbed my forehead, struggling to think straight. "I can send you money in a day or two for a hotel. But I can't come get you yet, I'm in Florida right now."

"What the hell are you doing down there?"

"Um, a job," I answered. It was close enough to the truth.

"If we scrape the money together, can we meet you down there?"

"No!" I barked louder than I had intended. "No, Jean. I'm sorry. I hate to be vague right now, but it's not safe for all of you here. I can't risk you or the kids."

"What the hell? Are you okay?"

"I'm fine, but... I'll have to explain it all later because it's too much for one phone call."

"Well, we might not have two days here, Mel." Jeanie's calmness cracked for just a second, but she recovered quickly. "They're trying not to kick three young kids out to the street, but they may not have a choice. People are already double-bunking and sleeping on the floor here."

"Shit." *Come on, Mel. There has to be a way.* But no clear solution came to me and I felt like I was failing them all over again.

"Babe." Connor sat next to me on the couch, looking at me with a soothing calmness. "If they need to get out now, I'll pick them up. I can take them to the house at the FDR Center and stay with them there until y'all take care of business down here."

My mouth dropped open to refuse, to say, *No, I need you here,* but I realized how selfish that was. My siblings were a day away from living on the street, and I was in a luxury suite overlooking Miami Beach. I had three other men here who would protect me with their lives, and Jeanie had no one.

So instead I asked, "Are you sure?"

He nodded. "Arjun is your best bet on beating this guy. The other two will help you win over the shifters too if need be. As the token human, I'm more likely to get in the way. But I'm there for your family, babe. They'll be safe and we'll wait for you to get back." He grabbed my hand and squeezed. "Because you *will* succeed and you *will* come back to us."

"Mel?" Jeanie asked. "Are you still there?"

"Hang on, Jean. I'm figuring something out." I muted the phone so she wouldn't hear us, then looked back at Connor. "You're absolutely positive you want to do this?"

"Yes, babe," he chuckled. "You don't need me to protect you, not like how you used to. You're a badass and you've got the other guys. But it sounds like your siblings need someone and I'm happy to be that person."

"If you're completely sure," I rested my forehead on his, "I can't thank you enough. I love you so much."

"No need to thank me. I take care of my woman and her people." He kissed me warmly. "When should I leave?"

"Right away. Like, now." I bit my lip. "They're in an overcrowded homeless shelter and could get kicked out at any time. They're in downtown Waterford, my hometown."

"I'll get the ol' bucket warmed up." He kissed me again as he rose from the couch. "Tell your sister I'm coming."

Releasing a breath, I unmuted the call. "Jean?"

"Yeah?"

"My, uh, boyfriend is coming to get you," I told her.

"He'll take you all to where we're staying and I'll meet you there after I'm done with the job here."

"Okay. That pale guy with the long hair I met?"

"No, that's Hunter," I said. "Connor is coming to get you. He'll show up in a big RV."

"Oh, damn. You're going through 'em fast." She was joking, but I heard the disapproval in her voice. Our mom went through boyfriends like bottles of Mickey's.

"No, it's not like that. I, ugh..." I pinched the bridge of my nose, not wanting to explain this to her now. "Hunter and I are still together, too. Everybody knows about each other. I'll explain later," I said lamely.

"Wait, what? You're with two guys?"

"Three, actually." And possibly a fourth, eventually.

"Mel, what the—"

"I'll explain later!" I couldn't help the giggle rising in my throat. "When I see you, which will be very soon. I promise, Jean."

"Mel, be honest with me. Are these guys—"

"Don't even finish that sentence," I told her. "They're great men. Amazing men, actually. They love me and want to protect me and my family. That's why Conner stepped up to get you. I trust them with my life. The little ones are in good hands with them, Jean. Connor won't let anything bad happen, I swear to you."

"Okay," she said after a long silence. "I believe you, sis."

"Thank you." I sighed a massive breath of relief. "Connor's leaving soon. He'll get there as soon as he can."

"Alright. I guess I'll see you soon."

"You definitely will," I told her. "And I'll explain everything when I see you guys. Give them kisses for me, I love you all."

"Love you, Mella!" the little ones shouted from the background before the line clicked dead.

"Goddamn, *steluţa.*"

I looked up, not even realizing that Hunter and Raz stood together in the kitchen the whole time.

"Guess everyone's awake," I muttered. "Did y'all here the whole thing?"

They nodded in unison. "Having Connor get them is smart," Hunter said.

"I agree," I said. "I just hate the idea of us being separated again, especially after you just got here."

"It won't be for long." Raz came up to me and pulled me into a strong embrace. "We'll string Lhozen up by his balls, free the shifters, and go home."

"If only it were that simple," I chuckled, laying my head on his shoulder.

"It definitely won't be."

The remark came from Arjun, who breezed out of his room and into the kitchen. "There's a high probability that my dear old stepfather will enslave or kill us all, and there will be no going home." He raised a glass of water with a bitter smile. "Cheers to us."

6

MELODY

"What should I tell them?"

I just shrugged and nuzzled my face harder into the center of Connor's chest. I didn't want him to leave me, as selfish as that was. He'd been at my side since the beginning. And now he was about to be hundreds of miles away. The RV's engine rumbled like a fearsome beast, echoing off the concrete walls of the hotel parking garage.

"They're going to see the pups, and Hunter's bros, and Miriam, most likely," he said, rubbing his hands down my back. "Your sister's going to ask questions and I'd rather not lie."

"Then tell them the truth," I answered, inhaling his sharp, masculine scent.

He squeezed around me tightly, dropping a kiss to the top of my head. "I'm gonna miss you, babe, but I'm not worried for once. Lhozen has no idea what's coming to him."

"It's the opposite," I groaned, placing my chin on his

chest to look up at him. "We have no idea what we're up against because everything is an illusion."

"You'll figure it out. You always do." He cupped my face, holding me in a long sensual kiss that I never wanted to end. "I gotta head out, babe," he murmured reluctantly, "if I'm gonna be there before tomorrow."

I nodded, slowly releasing my hold on him like we were stuck together with superglue. "Be safe. Tell them I love them and I'll see them soon."

"Absolutely." He kissed me again, a final time. "I love you, Mel. You better bring this sweet ass home to me."

"You know I will when you say shit like that." I laughed despite the dread in my chest and tears threatening to spill over. "I love you, Connor."

I stole one, two, three more last kisses before he bro-hugged all three other guys who stood around me, clapping each other hard on the back and exchanging well wishes. Hunter and Raz each held my hands as we watched Connor slowly back the RV out of its space. The tears didn't spill until he drove out of sight, and I could only hear the roar of the engine before it faded away.

Hunter and Raz held me between them as we got back in the elevator, kissing me and wiping my tears away. Arjun stood a polite distance away, looking in the opposite direction. All of us were silent as we came back to the suite. My tears dried quickly and a new feeling settled over me.

I had to do this. I had to beat him. Connor stepped up to do what he could. Now I had to do the same.

"Arjun."

"Yes, dove?" He turned to me with a curious look. He seemed to snap out of his shock from this morning, but I wondered if the uncertainty and doubts he expressed still weighed on him.

"What do I need to do?" I asked. "What is our best possible chance of taking him down?"

He took a deep breath. "Your Semblance needs to be at his level. You need to cast illusions not only over yourself but other people, objects, and locations. And they need to be strong enough to fool even him. That is our best possible chance."

"Okay. And how long will that take?"

"For an exceptionally gifted shaman as yourself?" He tapped his chin as he thought. "Years. Optimistically, three to five years if you practice daily."

"Years?!" I repeated, panic making my voice screech. "We don't have that kind of time!"

"Exactly," he said with mock cheer. "Therefore, we are well and truly fucked."

"What can you teach me in, like, two days?"

"Not anywhere close to enough," he replied. "You must understand, Mel, Lhozen has been a practicing shaman for over thirty years. Longer than any of us have been alive. And who knows how long he's held up the illusions around the compound. The longer they're cast, the more realistic they appear to be."

"So what can we do?" I cried with exasperation. "Besides give up?"

"I'll tell you what we *should* do," he said, his voice taking on a predatory growl. "Run down the street waving our arms in hopes that Connor sees us. We did our job. We've been paid. We went to the beach. The smartest thing we can do now is get the hell out and save our own arses."

I stared at him, half expecting him to morph into Lhozen himself or some other stranger, because it was the last thing I had expected Arjun to say.

"We can't leave," I said, fighting the tremble in my voice and the urge to scream. "They have no one to help them besides us. They need us. I promised Julian—"

"You should break that promise, dove. Won't be the worst thing in the world. He might even understand."

"Are you listening to yourself?" I demanded, my control shattering. "It already *is* the worst thing in the world for them, Arjun! They're suffering! They're dying! How can you say things like that when you went through the same?"

"You keep talking about *them*. I'm talking about *us!*" His words now echoed off the marble columns, as I could physically see his anger rising. Eyes wide, lips pulled back to show his teeth, fast movements meant to intimidate.

"Lhozen knows what Raz and I look like. He's probably waiting for all of us to waltz in on some daring, amateur rescue mission just so he can resell us. I'm not joking around, Mel. We *need* to save ourselves."

"We have to try." My teeth ground painfully against each other as I fought back the angry tears. "We can't just leave them."

"Mel, dove," he said in a gentler tone. "If you want to see Connor and your siblings again, then I'm afraid we must do exactly that."

"No," I crossed my arms defiantly. "There has to be a way we can save them *and* ourselves."

"What the fuck do you think I've been awake all night thinking about?!"

The outburst came from him so loud and suddenly, it

made me jump and shrink back. No one had yelled at me like that since I left home, and all my defensive instincts kicked in.

"Arj," Raz barked, stepping up to him and pressing a hand to his chest. "Take it easy, mate." Hunter approached him from my other side like a watchful bodyguard, golden eyes sharp.

The wound-up tiger shifter looked at each of them in turn before focusing on me again. "Mel, you have a good heart and you want to do right by the captive shifters. That's admirable," he said, sighing like he was tired. "But I know what Lhozen is capable of. We cannot win, dove. I'm sorry."

"Then why did you help me?" My voice cracked with helplessness. "Why even guide me through Speaking with them? We knew the risk was high. Why do all that just to give up now?"

He kept silent for a moment before lifting his eyes and saying sadly, "That was before I knew exactly who we were dealing with."

"So that's it, then?" My hands flopped to my sides. "Our ride just left and he's heading to Georgia. Not back here. So we're stuck here, anyway."

"You forget we have money now, Mel." The asshole dared to smirk. "We can catch a plane and be out of here in an hour."

I just shook my head. "I can't fucking believe you."

"It may be callous, yes." The smile dropped. "But Mel, it's the only way to preserve everything you've earned up until now. If Lhozen captures you, he will be the only shaman in the world with such a massive influence. You can do great things for shifters, but you must pick your battles."

A dry laugh escaped as I dropped my forehead into my hands. "And you don't stop rationalizing it. I really didn't expect this from you."

"What do you mean, Mel?"

I lifted my gaze back up to Arjun, then quickly turned toward the master bedroom. I couldn't stomach looking at him. I needed a pillow to punch and scream into.

"I never expected you to be such a fucking coward," I yelled over my shoulder before slamming the door.

7

ARJUN

I swirled the Scotch in my glass as I looked at the sunset over the beach. Our suite came well-stocked with expensive booze, but the Scotch just tasted like a bag of peat moss to me. I couldn't bring myself to enjoy anything after that argument with Mel.

She called me a coward, then stormed off to her room hours ago. And here I was, hoping to enjoy the sunset with some company. Maybe even have a chance to finish that kiss so rudely interrupted this morning.

And now the chances of that were essentially zero.

I didn't enjoy upsetting her. I especially hated seeing the heartbreak on her face when I told her we should leave. But it was the cold, uncomfortable truth as far as I could see. We couldn't save everyone. But we might be able to save a few more if we survived ourselves.

It was an argument that would've kept us going around in circles. At this point, she must've seen me as utterly selfish. And I couldn't understand how she could be so bloody selfless. How had she not gotten herself killed yet? Or gotten someone else killed? She wanted to storm into battle like the most ill-equipped soldier and yell, "Freedom!" at the top of her lungs while getting hacked to death. No thanks.

The sliding door opened behind me and I immediately picked up Razvan's smoky scent.

"Not having a romantic evening with your mates?" I asked.

"Eh," he muttered, leaning his forearms on the balcony railing beside me. "The mood isn't very romantic right now."

"Wonder why." I stared into my glass. "So are you here to convince me we should die as shifter-heroes that no one will remember?"

"I'm not here to convince you of anything," the dragon replied briskly. "I see your point. I see hers too. But we have to come to a decision, one way or the other."

"Explain her view to me, then." My hand tightened around my Scotch glass until it was nearly painful. "Is she just suicidal? Does she want to let the enslaved shifters see a friendly face before they're all dead?"

"She's a rescuer," he said with an easygoing shrug. "If someone is suffering, she has to help them. It's that simple."

"But it's *not* that simple. Surely she must see that?" I downed the rest of the glass, choking it back. I didn't care much for Scotch after seeing how much Lhozen depended on it after Mum died. Still, I needed something to take the edge off before I lost my shit again.

"She understands that, logically," Raz replied. "It doesn't matter to her, though. If someone needs her help, she will give it to them. It's just how she is."

"But why?" I tore my fingers through my hair, endlessly frustrated by this woman. "Why can't she think about preserving her own life for one damn second?"

"My guess is because of how she was raised," he mused. "She never had the luxury of taking care of herself. Since she was a child, taking care of others always fell on her. Walking away from it all and joining her first carnival was probably the only selfish thing she ever did. And even then, she did it to find a way to support her siblings." He shot me a sheepish grin. "That's what I think, anyway. Connor could probably tell you more and in a much better way."

"No, that makes a lot of sense, actually," I sighed, feeling the anger leave like letting the air out of a balloon. "What if I wasn't here, Raz? You went through the same shit as me. Would you go along with her on a rescue mission or try to talk her out of it?"

"I'd go with her," he replied without an ounce of hesitation. "Not because it's the best thing to do, necessarily. But if no one goes with her, she'll do it alone. And I'd never save my own skin to leave her behind."

"Because you're in love with her," I stated. "Of course you wouldn't."

"Even if I wasn't," his eyes bore into mine, "you don't just let someone walk into danger like that. I don't think you're a coward, mate, but that shit *is*. I'll turn the question back on you. What if *I* wasn't here? Nor Hunter? Would you let her walk into the compound by herself? Because that's exactly what she'll do."

"No," I muttered. "But I'd stop her before she got anywhere near it. Maybe tie her up if I had to."

My cock swelled unexpectedly, and I turned to subtly

adjust it. Just a flashing image of Mel, naked, tied, and writhing on a bed, sent my tiger roaring. *Yes, she is our mate. We must take her!*

No. No, she's not. We must remember that.

Thankfully, Raz didn't seem to notice.

"That might not work." His mouth lifted into a smirk. "She's a tricky one."

"Whatever. I'd prevent it from happening and force her to watch videos on the importance of self-preservation. Put your own air mask on before helping others, that kind of thing."

"It won't matter," he said softly. "It's in her blood."

"Well, if she nearly gets herself killed another time, she may think twice and thank me."

"Arjun, man." Raz stared at me with a slight shake of his head. "Do you even know why you're fighting her so hard on this?"

"Because I'm trying to keep us alive, Raz." I returned his stare. "That's what I've been bloody saying this whole time."

"That's not the only reason," he breathed. "You're fighting your feelings for her, too."

"Oh, for fuck's sake..."

I turned to head back inside, thoroughly done with this bullshit psychoanalysis, but Raz caught my arm. And I couldn't find it in myself to fight him as well.

"You see it now, you big pussy?" He pulled me back to the railing with a shit-eating grin. "You see why we're all crazy about her because you are too."

"I am not. That's ridiculous."

"Arjun." He said my name slowly, like trying to placate a child. "It's okay. You're already one of us, anyway."

"I don't want to be like... that."

"Sharing her." He nodded knowingly. "I understand it's weird to think about. Especially with your upbringing. But you know us all, mate. We get along and we all just want her safe and happy. And she's so giving, so loving. You know she does all she can to make us happy, too. You can see that."

"I've heard quite enough of this bollocks."

I pushed off the railing, and this time he didn't try to pull me back. The animal inside me only roared and pawed at the edges of my human skin. He agreed with the dragon and found it infuriating that I was resisting. *She is our mate! We must take her! Her other mates have given permission.*

It took all my willpower to hold him back. When I reached my room, I even checked the mirror to make sure I hadn't partially shifted.

All I could do was pace, well, like a caged animal. She felt right. She smelled right. It wasn't just my tiger side that wanted to make her mine. And if I asked myself honestly, I didn't even mind sharing her with the other men.

But to love such a stubborn woman hellbent on saving all shifter-kind, was to surely lose her.

❧ 8 ❧

MELODY

"I'm hungry," I whined, rolling over so my head rested on Hunter's stomach.

"Hi, Hungry. I'm Hunter," he snorted, tickling my side.

"Leave it you to make dad jokes," I giggled, squirming away.

"Want to go out for dinner?" He ran his fingers over my calf and I shivered under the touch. "Or get something delivered?"

I looked up at him. "Arjun is probably still out there, isn't he?"

He gave me a pointed look and tapped his index finger on my nose. "You'll have to face him eventually, little fox."

"I don't wanna," I sighed. "He's the only one who can help with my abilities, but won't. Just thinking about it pisses me off."

"If you think about it another way, he cares enough about you—about all of us—to not want to risk our lives."

"By walking away from those who are already *at* risk!"

"I know, love." He dropped a kiss to my nose. "I'm just saying, I see his perspective too."

I laced my fingers through his and held our hands over my belly. Where I possibly had a child growing.

No, don't think about that.

"What do you think I should do?" I looked up at my wolf. "Is it really stupid of me to even attempt this?"

"Of course I don't think you're stupid." He raised our hands off my belly and kissed the back of my palm. "It's important to look at all the risks and try to mitigate as many as possible, but I think you should do what feels right."

"I just know doing nothing is wrong."

"Then nothing is what we won't do."

"What?" I looked up at him, unable to hold back my giggle.

"Don't not laugh at my double-negative," he teased, tickling my sides again before swatting my hip. "Come on. Let's get food, then figure out how we're going to rescue some shifters."

I stalled, dragged my feet, and whined some more. We eventually left the bedroom to find Raz in the living room, alone. He had his feet up on the coffee table, flipping through the TV channels with a bored expression on his face. When we came out, his eyes lit up.

"Hey, my loves," he greeted us, accepting a kiss from Hunter first, and then me as if we hadn't seen each other in days rather than the past hour.

"Hungry, Raz?" Hunter called from the kitchen, flipping through various menus while I slid in next to our dragon.

"Always," he replied, draping an arm over my shoulders and pulling me into his side.

"What're you in the mood for?"

"A sandwich," I blurted out, much to their amusement.

"God, you're insatiable, and I love it," Raz growled with a nuzzle to my cheek.

"Little fox, I'm still recovering from last night." Hunter came up behind the couch and pressed a kiss to my other cheek. "You can have a sandwich later, though," he added in a seductive whisper before returning to the kitchen.

"Worth a try," I sighed, stretching my legs over Raz's lap. A sudden pang of missing Connor hit me squarely in the chest at that moment. He usually had my legs, while Raz supported my back.

My dragon must have noticed the sudden shift in my demeanor. He cupped my chin, turning my gaze to meet his.

"We'll be with him soon, *steluța*," he assured me, pulling me snugly into his lap. "Our big happy family will be even bigger and happier after our work is done."

"I wish he didn't have to leave," I admitted. "Of course, I don't want my siblings to be homeless, but he'd be able to see something I can't. We could use an extra brain to figure out how the hell to get into this place and get everyone out."

"*Steluța*," Raz said with a gentle tone that almost sounded scolding. "You would not have gotten off the phone with your sister saying there was nothing you could do. That's not how you are."

"I know, of course not. Shit, I'd probably go pick them up myself, but—"

"You made the best choice for them," he said softly.

"Now we have to decide how to proceed with the resources we have left."

"Which is apparently nowhere," I said with an exaggerated look around the suite. "Did he up and leave already?"

"Arjun? He's brooding in his room again." Raz frowned. "He wouldn't just leave, you know that."

"That's not what he said this morning," I huffed.

Before Raz could reply, the sound of Arjun's door opening reached every corner of the living room like an omen. Even Hunter paused in flipping through the takeout menus.

The tiger shifter emerged from his cave, shoulders square and moving stiffly as he headed for the armchair next to our couch. He sat down mechanically, staring at his tented fingers and resting his forearms on his knees.

"To cast Semblance on something besides yourself, you need to start with small details that you can focus on," he said abruptly. "Your focus is what holds those illusions and makes them believable. Something like eye or hair color."

"Wait, hold the phone," I held up a hand. "What's going on here?"

"From what your mates tell me, and what I've gathered from our... conversation this morning," he lifted his gaze coolly to me. "You will insist on carrying out this rescue mission despite the heavily stacked odds against you and us. So I will teach you to cast better, more effective illusions in order to make this slightly less of a suicide mission."

"So... you'll help me?" I asked in disbelief after a long silence.

He shrugged. "My guidance in the limited time we have won't get you very far. But again, if you must put yourself and those you love in danger, I might as well give you a chance to say goodbye before you meet your end." He straightened up to look at Hunter in the kitchen. "Now, how about some tea, then? Actually, never mind," he rose from the armchair, "I'll get it myself."

Once he was settled in with his tea and Hunter called in our dinner order for delivery, I drilled him with questions.

"So I can cast illusions that aren't... shifter-related?" I wasn't sure what to call it. Up until that point, I only knew how to give myself shifter features like Razvan's dragon horns or Hunter's teeth. While seeing through the eyes of a fox shifter once, Raz had caught me with furry, red ears on top of my head.

"It's possible, yes," he replied after a hearty sip of tea. "It depends on the shaman and how strong their innate Semblance ability is. Lhozen's was always exceptional. He pranked me often by creating doors and such that weren't really there. The more complex an illusion you're casting, the more skill and focus it takes, which is why I suggest starting small."

"Like hair or eye color," I repeated, focusing on the depths of Arjun's irises. In my head I pictured the endless blueish-green darkening to a warm chocolate brown like my own. It was a feature I knew well and figured it would be the easiest to try out.

"Whoa! Arjun, holy shit!" Raz leaned forward, squinting like he couldn't make sense of what he saw. "Look in the mirror, mate."

Arjun obliged, standing to look at his reflection in the gilded mirror next to the door. "Ah. Well done," he said, sounding unimpressed. He still looked handsome. Dark eyes suited his complexion well, but he didn't have that breath-taking brightness to his face without his natural eye color.

"That was clearly easy for you, so you can drop the illusion now and try something more difficult," he said, returning to his seat.

"Hm." I tapped my finger on my chin, feeling sassy. "I don't know. Maybe I'll keep it up and see how much my focus can shift. You said the longer the illusion remains, the more realistic it becomes, right?"

He glared at me, which no longer seemed as intimidating with dark eyes. "Yes, the longer you keep an illusion up, the less focus you need. Your train of thought is correct."

I returned his glare with a smile, enjoying myself perhaps a little too much. "Don't worry, Arjun. I'll give you your eyes back. Just let me test what else I can do."

"Alright," he grumbled a little petulantly. "Keep my eyes the color of shit while you do something else. Give Hunter a perm, maybe."

I ignored his dig at my eye color and looked at Raz instead, a different idea forming in my mind.

"Oh no. What's that look for?" he teased, gray eyes twinkling with curiosity.

My eyelids closed halfway to concentrate as I pictured him in my mind while still keeping awareness of Arjun's new eye color.

"Holy shit!" Hunter exclaimed from the kitchen, coming up behind the couch in two long strides. He tugged at Raz's collar to get a better look at his neck, wide golden eyes traveling all over our dragon. "Raz, look at your hands."

Holding his palms out in front of his face, Raz nearly jumped out of his now un-tattooed skin when he saw them.

"What the..." He lifted his shirt to reveal smooth, unblemished skin without a drop of ink in sight.

"Look in the mirror, mate," Arjun couldn't hold back his laugh. "You look like a damn church boy."

I watched him get up and look, holding the illusion with relative ease as he stared at himself, touching his face, turning around, even undoing his pants to see that his more adventurous tattoos and piercings were gone.

"*Steluţa*, why would you do this to me?" he lamented, although he shot me a playful smirk in the mirror's reflection.

"I've wondered what you looked like with naked skin," I shrugged. Like Arjun, he still looked sexy as hell without his tattoos, just different. My illusions took away their uniqueness in a way and made them more normal, if even a bit bland. My dragon just wasn't himself without all his ink.

"I've been getting tattoos since I was thirteen. I would never look like this," he said, still looking at himself in disbelief.

"Let's hope Lhozen thinks that too," I replied. "By the way, open your mouth."

He obliged, wiggling a now perfectly intact tongue at the mirror.

"Now I know you won't keep that illusion up," he grinned, turning to face me. "You enjoy my tongue too much."

I nearly shrank back under his gaze. The illusion was

almost too real already. It felt like a stranger was looking at me too suggestively.

"Let's move on," Arjun snapped. "Now, you'll also need to disguise inanimate objects. You can make them look like something else or disappear entirely. This should be easier than creating illusions over people, since objects are more simple to create and manipulate. Try making the coffee table disappear."

I did so easily. I also turned it into a billiards table when he asked. And then turned the couch into a hot tub and made that disappear. I turned the ceiling lights into elaborate chandeliers and the floor tiles into plush carpet. And on and on and on for what felt like hours. Everything Arjun told me to do, I did. All the while, I kept up the illusion of his brown eyes and Razvan's choir boy look.

By the time he told me to turn an end table into a fire pit with the illusion of heat as well, my focus faltered and my head began to pound painfully.

I rubbed my temples as I curled up on the couch. Strong arms pulled me into an embrace, and a soothing kiss dropped to my forehead.

"Well done, little fox," Hunter murmured. "Looks like you're about tapped out."

"I've never seen anything like that." Raz curled up behind me, his now-tattooed hands and arms wrapping around me. "You really are fucking magical."

"She's going to need to do a lot more if we have any chance of beating Lhozen," Arjun said snappily. I cracked an eye open to see that his ocean-colored irises had returned, and they captured me from across the room. "Sure, you're exceptionally gifted, Mel. But look how drained you are. To Lhozen, everything we did just now would be child's play. Our chances of beating him are still slim to none."

"Hey, that's enough," Hunter barked with a soft warning growl. "She's doing the best she can. You can only push her to do so much."

"He's right, Arj," Raz added. "You can't force her to be powerful enough to win in a single day."

"Guys, it's okay," I said, sitting up between them and looking at Arjun. "Thank you. Seriously."

His eyebrows lifted in surprise. All three guys just looked at me like I sprouted an extra head, so I elaborated.

"I don't want you to go easy on me. I don't want any sugar-coating on how hard this is going to be. I might not be as powerful as him, but I want to go in as prepared as possible, and that means my limits need to be tested. So thank you, Arjun, for pushing me to my limit and not holding back."

Again, no one said anything. But Arjun inclined his head toward me in a sign that he understood and that was plenty enough for me.

CONNOR

I parked the RV in a lot across the street from the shelter and hopped out, keeping my guard up and taking in my surroundings as I jaywalked to the front entrance. It was only two blocks away from the main downtown strip, with trendy restaurants and shops, but far enough that it seemed like an entirely different country.

Giant trees lined the block, cracking and uprooting the street and sidewalks. Clearly, the city hadn't bothered to come out and trim them in years. The rundown state of the houses and yards showed barely any care or money went into them. This area of Mel's hometown was just as forgotten and crumbling as her old trailer park.

The homeless shelter itself looked like a large house that was one storm away from crumbling to the ground. It had no signage and looked completely unassuming next to the other houses on the block. Mel told me it catered toward women and kids escaping abusive situations, which explained why it was kept hidden like this.

I entered the front door to be immediately met with a suspicious glare from a woman sitting behind a desk.

"Can I help you?" she asked shrewdly.

"Good evening, ma'am." I offered her a smile, which she didn't return. "I'm here to see Miss Jeanie May."

"Is she expecting you?"

"Yes, ma'am, she is."

"Are you family?" Her eyes narrowed at me. "How do you know her?"

"I'm her sister's boyfriend. My name is Connor Shaw. We've arranged for Jeanie and the younger ones to stay with us."

"Why isn't her sister with you?"

"Melody couldn't get away from work," I explained. It was mostly true. "I'll be happy to wait, ma'am, while you verify everything with Jeanie."

I took a seat on a folding chair near the door, trying to keep my posture relaxed while still alert. I understood why they were suspicious of men coming here, but the suspicious looks and questioning still irked me just a little. Whether on my legs or my gender, it felt like I was going to be judged no matter what.

The woman blinked in apparent surprise, like I was one of the few guys who didn't throw a fit at the immediate suspicion.

"I'll be right back." She rose from her desk, never taking her eyes off me as she slipped through another door.

Once alone, I leaned my head back with a sigh to rest it on the wall. It had been barely twelve hours, and I already missed Mel something fierce. The world felt so different without the one person who accepted all of me at my side.

A good ten minutes passed before the door opened again and a teenage girl stepped out. She had strawberry blonde hair up in a messy bun and crystal blue eyes, but her nose and face shape were nearly identical to Mel's.

"You're Connor?" she asked in a small voice.

"Yes, ma'am." I stood from the chair. "You're Jeanie, I presume."

She nodded, those large eyes studying me from the doorway as if surveying a threat.

"If there's anything you want to know, ask me." I spread my hands out, palms open. "I know I'm a stranger to you, and it's a lot to ask for you to come with me. I don't want you to be afraid."

"No matter what I ask, you could just lie," she pointed out.

I held back a smile. She had the same fire as Mel.

"But my sister trusts you," she added. "That's the best assurance I'm going to get. So let me pack up the kids and our stuff."

I nodded, feeling a huge swell of relief in my chest that I wouldn't have to convince her to come with me. "Y'all need any help?"

"No. I'll be right back." She went back through the door and returned a few minutes later, holding a curly-haired toddler on her hip. Her other hand gently guided two other children, a boy and a girl, in front of her.

They all looked completely different, but with enough similarities that you could guess they were related. The three younger children openly stared at me with wide-eyed curiosity.

"Hi, guys." I lowered to a squat to be at their eye level. "My name's Connor. I'm a friend of your sister, Mel. We're gonna see her real soon, okay?"

"Mella?" the dark-haired girl piped up. "We gonna see Mella?" Only when she looked straight at me did I notice the faint bruising around her eye. Like a reflex, my fist clenched at my side, but I put on my best non-threatening smile for her.

"That's right, little lady. What are your names?"

As they often did, the kids went shy and clung to Jeanie's legs as they looked up at her.

"This is Bella," she introduced, putting her hand on the dark-haired girl's shoulder. "She likes to rhyme with her name, so she calls Mel Mella. This is Joey." She ruffled the hair of the boy with medium brown hair.

"He's Jella," Bella giggled.

"And this is Riley," Jeanie bounced the toddler girl on her hip. "Say hi to Connor. He's a friend."

Riley just smiled shyly and buried her face in Jeanie's neck.

"Nice to meet all of you. And you can call me Connella if you want," I said to Bella, who giggled into her hand. "If y'all are ready," I said to Jeanie, rising back up to my feet. "The sooner we go, the sooner we can get y'all set up."

"Ready when you are," she nodded curtly. "We don't have much. Kinda had to get out of there in a hurry."

Just then I noticed she, Bella, and Joey carried small, worn-out backpacks and nothing else. After hearing everything Mel said about her life growing up, they probably didn't own much more than that.

"Alright, I'm just parked across the street. It's an RV, so there's plenty of room. Are y'all hungry?"

"We just had dinner, so we should be good," Jeanie answered, following my lead with the kids in tow.

"Sounds good. We can stop anytime on the way. Just let me know."

All five of us barely made it out the front door and onto the sidewalk when Bella screamed and immediately began crying and babbling hysterically. Concerned, I turned to her and kneeled down. I didn't notice the man approaching until her small, shaking hand lifted and pointed over my shoulder.

"Shit," Jeanie hissed, pulling the kids close. "I knew he'd find us."

The guy was about my height, bow-legged and with a beer gut hanging over his pants. He swung his arms as he walked, bald head forward and beady eyes narrowed. This motherfucker was looking for a fight.

"Relax," I murmured, rising up to standing. "I got this. Y'all go back inside for now."

"Inside?" she asked. "But what're you—"

"Just in case it gets ugly, the little ones shouldn't see this. Hopefully, it won't get to that. Now go on."

"Connor, he's—"

"Jeanie. Inside," I said, raising my voice just slightly.

She listened that time, dragging the kids back through the front door and slamming it shut just as the shithead stopped in front of the house. And me.

"Fuckin' move, asshole," he grunted at me, his speech slurring.

"Nah, man," I replied with a calm that I must've channeled from Hunter, folding my arms in front of my chest. "That ain't gonna happen."

He got in my face, forcing me to hold my breath

against the rank smell coming from him. "I dunno who the fuck you are, but you need to mind your own fuckin' business. Those are my kids in there and I'm gonna take their ungrateful asses home."

"Funny. They don't look too eager to go home with you." I lifted an eyebrow. "I wonder why that is. Something to do with the little girl's bruise, I bet?" I knew I was goading him but I couldn't help it. What kind of disgusting piece of shit came to a homeless shelter drunk like this?

"I told you to mind your own fuckin' business!" His hands shot out and gave a weak shove to my shoulders. Even if I didn't have awesome balance on these new legs, he had no power behind his push and I remained standing like a boulder. The guy looked intimidating enough to go around picking fights, but he was fucking weak. Apparently, nobody had put him in his place before.

"Look, man. You're lucky I'm a nice guy," I said, keeping my voice calm despite the rage simmering underneath. "But if you touch me again, you'll wish you never came here looking for a fight. This ain't the place for that, so I'm giving you this one chance to turn around and leave."

"Fuck no, I'm not leavin'! Those kids are my fuckin paycheck, so they're comin' the fuck home! And I'm givin' you this one chance to get the fuck out of my way! Who the fuck are you, anyway?" he sneered at me. "You fuckin' Jeanie? I knew that dumb bitch had a sugar daddy."

"Changed my mind." I smiled cheerily at him. "You don't get another chance." With that, I drove my metallic foot straight up between his legs, connecting with soft flesh.

His mouth dropped open to scream, but only a pathetic whimper escaped. He held himself as he doubled over, slowly crumpling to the ground as the pain set in. I actually put some effort behind that kick, so I was pretty sure I ruptured at least one of his testes.

I pushed open the front door of the shelter, meeting four pairs of wide eyes.

"Coast is clear. Let's go," I said.

"What did you do?" Jeanie demanded, holding the young ones tightly as we walked past the guy, rolling around on the sidewalk in pain.

"Don't worry, he won't go picking fights again," I told her. "And I'm pretty sure he won't be able to have any more kids."

"He's acting like a baby," Bella laughed.

"I called the cops," Jeanie said, tugging Bella's hand to keep her close as we crossed the street.

"Oh, good," I said cheerfully, looking both ways for traffic. "He can tell them whatever he wants."

We boarded the RV, and I started it up while Jeanie secured the kids. When she buckled up in the passenger seat next to me, I paused before putting it in drive.

"Any other loose ends to tie up?" I asked her.

She looked at me and gave an emphatic shake of her head.

"Nope. Get us the fuck out of there."

❦   10   ❧

ARJUN

Mel grasped Semblance faster than any of Lhozen's students that I'd ever seen. It wasn't easy, and I could see how much effort she put into practicing the illusions. It made me respect her even more, though I found myself constantly shoving it down and giving her even more to do.

Under any other circumstances, it was too much. She was mentally and physically exhausted, and I just kept pushing her. But she never asked for a break. She never wanted to stop. Whenever Raz or Hunter suggested she take it easy, she just demanded more. *What next, Arjun?* she asked, her brows knitted with the headache she surely felt. And so I kept giving her more illusions to practice.

I kept hurting her when all I wanted to do was hold her.

After an evening of practicing in the suite, we upped the ante the next morning. She cast illusions over Raz and Hunter, giving them disguises so they could scope out La Hacienda. This time, they'd hang out in the cafe across the street and watch how people entered and left the compound.

For today's illusions, she erased Raz's tattoos again and gave him dark eyes and curly brown hair. She made Hunter a foot shorter and slightly overweight, with darkened features and hazel eyes. They were both so normal and average-looking, no one would give them a second glance. Even my cynical arse had to admit their disguises were good.

"Remember, the illusion is only a shift in perception, not reality," I told her when they left. "Hunter still *feels* tall, and he is. If someone touches him above his illusion's head, they'll feel the real Hunter's body. The risk is always there. Even humans may be able to see through your illusion, the perceptive ones anyway."

"Connor would," she sighed wistfully. "I wonder how he's doing. He should have picked up my siblings by now."

"Don't let yourself get distracted," I warned. My tiger yearned to comfort her, to rub his big striped face against her side and let her be soothed by his purr. I fought him down, despite those instincts feeling like they were taking over me with each passing day.

"Keep your focus."

She nodded, her eyes half-closing as she resumed concentrating on Raz and Hunter's illusions. Weeks, maybe even days ago, she would have rolled her eyes and gotten huffy with me. I would've said some remark that made her bristle and she'd storm off to one of her mates with a red face and a stick up her arse.

Now, her back straightened, and her chin lifted. She trusted my word and never once complained. Even with no formal training at all, she looked like a proud shaman.

Like the ones Lhozen used to tell me about in my childhood.

I shook my head at the memory and stared out the window at the ocean, partially so Mel wouldn't catch me staring. Also, because I still couldn't reconcile the man who raised me with the monster who kidnapped shifters for profit.

Was it all a lie? That was the question that I kept coming back to and had no answer for. For as long as I could remember, he took me to school every day. He encouraged me to read and think critically, even with things I didn't agree with. He adored my mother and treated her with the utmost respect. Was it losing her that triggered this shift?

If by some miracle of Shiva we survived this and had him at our mercy, he could not be allowed to live. It was the one thing I was sure of in this whole mess.

A soft thump prompted my head to swivel back to Mel, who had slumped over on her side. Her head leaned against the armrest of the couch, her half-closed eyelids fluttering rapidly.

Before I could control myself, my legs carried me to her, and I gently leaned her back upright.

"Here, dove," I murmured, taking a seat next to her and allowing her to lie back down again with her head in my lap. I stroked her hair away from her face. Not knowing what else to do in this intimate position I found myself in, I allowed my tiger to purr at the contact with her.

She smiled dreamily, resting her hand on my thigh near her face. "You're being nice, now. I never know when I'm going to get nice Arjun or grumpy Arjun."

My chest felt tight, and I swallowed a dry lump in my throat. Even now, she could be lighthearted and sweet.

"I have been hard on you, and wish I could take it all back now," I confessed. "You shouldn't bear the burden of this alone. I know him better than anyone. It should be me carrying the weight of this plan."

"Stop, Arjun," she murmured, tightening her hand ever so slightly around my thigh. Regardless of her gentle grip, it sent a rush of heat and desire straight to my cock. "I have to do this because I'm the only shaman among us."

"I know," I sighed. "And you're an incredible shaman. Not just because of your abilities, but what you're using them for. I haven't told you that enough."

"It's because of you. Don't you realize that?" she gazed up at me. "If it wasn't for you, I wouldn't know how to block the shifters out when we first came here. I'd have one hell of a concussion, and that is, if I didn't die from trying to make it stop. You gave me the mental shields to deal with them."

"You had them all along." I gave her a weak smile. "I just helped you find them."

"Arjun." She sat up, now incredibly close to me. We'd been in close proximity before, but not like this. Her hand still rested on my thigh. "Where is all this humility coming from?" She allowed a tiny smirk on those rosebud lips. "It's not like you to be humble."

Unlike her, I couldn't find the humor in this situation. Not right now.

"When we get in there," I said, "I'm going to have to face him. Me and no one else. And I'll have to ask him why." I looked away from her, returning my gaze to the ocean. "I have to know, for my own peace of mind, why he did this to me? To Raz and all the others. Guessing is driving me insane."

"I understand," she whispered. "And it's because of you we have a fighting chance of getting in there at all. Don't diminish your role in this, Arjun. None of it would be possible without you."

"I have to kill him." I returned my gaze to her, fighting the urge to look away. She was just too lovely. "You realize that, right? Once I have my answer, I have to do it. And it has to be me and no one else."

Her expression flickered before returning to its blank gaze of concentration, and she nodded. "I do understand, and I won't stop you. I'm sure everyone in that place will want the same thing, but you're right. It has to be you."

"The thing is, Mel," I covered her hand with my own, wrapping my fingers tightly around hers. "I don't know if I can do it."

She looked at me as if about to say something, then did the complete opposite of what I expected. She kissed me.

It took me by surprise, but I kissed her back as if I'd been waiting to do so for years. And truthfully, maybe I had been.

Her arms wrapped around my neck and my tiger released a growl of pleasure at the sensation of her nails running across my scalp. She tasted perfect, absolutely delicious. Her mouth opened up to me delicately and let out the softest moan at my invading tongue, claiming her.

Just as quickly as she started, she broke away.

"Sorry." Her breath came out in soft pants. "I was doing good for a while but started to lose focus."

I could only blink at her, my brain trying to catch up and reconcile what just happened. She sat halfway in my lap, her fingers in my hair. Her chest pressed to mine, my arms holding her there and wrapping around her back. I could still taste her on my mouth and I was hard as a steel beam.

"The guys are talking to me up here," she tapped her temple, smiling shyly with her cheeks flushed pink. "Raz saw one of his hand tattoos coming back and let me know."

"Right," I cleared my throat. "How are they doing?"

"Good. They're noticing a pattern with how people are entering and leaving the compound. No one has given them any extra attention."

"Good. Yes, that is good." Apparently, kissing her had robbed my brain's capacity for everything but repeating the same words.

We sat like that for an incredibly awkward amount of time. When she pressed her forehead to mine, my hand drifted up to brush her hair off her shoulder. Her soft lips skimmed a trail down my cheek, breath gently fanning across my skin. My heart crashed like a drum as she inched closer to my mouth.

"I thought you needed to focus," I murmured, my lips just barely in contact with hers.

"I am," she replied playfully, pressing another kiss to the corner of my mouth. "But I also need my focus tested by distractions, so..."

Gods above, I didn't want to fight this anymore. Clearly, neither did she. Still, I had to, albeit for different reasons than before.

"You don't want to make a habit of this, dove," I murmured, turning my face away.

"Why not?" The rejection in her voice was like broken

glass in my skin. "The guys have talked to me about this. I'm sure they have with you, too. Arjun, is it—"

"Your heart is too big," I told her, carefully sliding her off my lap. "Too pure. I can't be the one to break it. I'm sorry, Mel. It has nothing to do with sharing you, but I can't do this."

"Then what's the matter?" she demanded. I hated myself for causing the pain she felt at that moment, but it would be better in the long run. It killed me to refuse her, but I'd always choose that over breaking her heart later.

"Lhozen," I said, barely above a whisper. "He's more likely to kill me than I am to kill him."

MELODY

After watching the hidden entrance to the compound outside of La Hacienda for most of the day, Raz and Hunter felt confident they knew how to get in.

Arjun and I mostly avoided each other after the awkwardness on the couch. He gave me tips on holding up the illusions from across the suite, and I took his advice while doing other things to distract myself in order to test my focus.

When housekeeping came, I turned them away and cleaned the place myself, only staying out of Arjun's room. The master bed and bath were immaculate. I swept and swiffered the marble floors until they were spotless. It was incredibly tempting to hide under the bed out of shame and embarrassment from Arjun rejecting me.

My thoughts and emotions were so mixed up, it was all I could do to keep Raz and Hunter's disguises up as they made their way back to the hotel. I wanted to call bullshit on Arjun's excuse, though he had no reason to lie to me. As far as I knew, he had never lied to me once.

Deep down, I knew the truth of it was I didn't want to believe Lhozen could kill him. I didn't want to face the fact I was bringing three amazing men to their possible deaths. Knowing that, how could I carry this out? Was I just kidding myself on this rescue mission like what Arjun had been telling me all along?

You can't just stumble around and figure your way out of this one, I told myself. This isn't some shitty carnival anymore. All of our lives are at risk.

A click followed by the sound of a door opening let me know that my boys had returned.

"*Steluța!*" Even Raz's voice sounded different. "Please drop the illusions now, I feel like the victim of a damn body snatcher."

Letting go of that concentration felt like an enormous weight off my mind. My wolf and my dragon, now with their familiar handsome faces, wandered into the bedroom.

"Why're you hiding in here, little fox?" Hunter asked with a curious look at me. Those sharp eyes missed nothing.

"How did it go?" I stood from the bed to greet them both with kisses, purposely ignoring his question.

"Perfectly," Raz answered with pride. "No one suspected a thing and we've got the entryway down. It seems like not all the compound workers fully grasp the illusions, so we even have a bit of wiggle room when we attempt to get in."

"How are you?" Hunter tugged me against him possessively. "Everything okay while we were gone?"

"Yeah," I sighed. "Took some Midol for the headaches. I'm just a little foggy right now."

"Does that have anything to do with Arjun?" Hunter kissed the top of my head before I looked up at him. How did he know?

"I can smell him on you," the smug wolf answered.

"And it's clear you're avoiding him," Raz added.

Damn them. It must've been Connor's influence, making them so perceptive. The thought only made my chest ache for my Marine even more.

"I kissed him," I admitted. "And he rejected me after that."

"Oh, my love. Don't let him get to you." Raz stepped into Hunter's embrace around me and gave me the most passionate, reassuring kiss I needed. "If he kisses you too much, he'll feel compelled to marry you next. It's just the way he is."

"He did mention that." I remembered our walk on the beach a few days ago. He came from a culture of arranged marriages and all intimacy happening behind closed doors. It was difficult for me to see from that perspective, especially since I was so open and affectionate with my three. But I *wanted* to understand him. I wanted him to know I accepted all his quirks, just like the other guys.

"In any case, it's probably best to worry about this if we're still alive after tomorrow," I muttered.

"We will be," Hunter said firmly. "Not one of us can do it alone, but the four of us can manage together. And you've got your Marine and your siblings to see after this is over."

"You're right," I breathed, leaning my ear against his heart. "Surviving is the only option."

The next morning, all four of us met in the living room and went over our plan. I slept like the dead the previous night and still felt groggy until I got some coffee and breakfast in me. Raz and Hunter filled us in on how to get inside, and Arjun made sure to repeat our plan several times.

"Mel." His gaze lasered in on me. "You're the only one who's seen the inside. We're essentially going in blind and you have to be on top of your Semblance. If your focus wavers just a little, it could be the end for us. If you have any doubts about this, please let us know now."

"No doubts," I told him. "I won't let any of you be discovered."

"It's not just keeping up the illusions," he said. "You'll be right at the source of all the visions that have plagued you since we left home. Since they appear to get stronger the closer you are, you'll have to block all of them too." The intensity of his gaze softened, along with his voice. "A lot is riding on your shoulders, dove. I wish we could do more, but we all have to count on you."

His words echoed the sentiment of what he had said last night, right before our kiss. He didn't want me carrying the lion's share of this mission, but there was no way around it. Only I could cast the illusions to get us inside. The guys' muscle might help us once we were in, but we truly didn't know.

I felt the yearning from him like it was my own. Maybe it was his manly pride wanting to step up and do more, or possibly his feelings for me. Though I still had no idea what those honestly entailed. My own feelings were a swirling mix of confusion. The kiss felt more than good. It felt right.

But I had to focus on the life-or-death situation at hand.

"I understand," I told him flatly. "I can't pretend to know if I'll be able to do both at once, but my number one priority is to keep y'all hidden and safe. Even if the shifters get through my mind, I'll be focusing on you guys no matter what."

Arjun gave a curt nod, the other two said nothing. I could only imagine what they were thinking. Maybe they just wanted to go home too. To live happily ever after as freed shifters despite so many others trapped in the same situation they had once been in. Maybe it was selfish of me to drag them into this just, because I couldn't stand to see suffering. People and animals would always suffer. It was part of living after all.

But if I *could* do something about it, then why wouldn't I?

And if I was lucky enough to find one, let alone three or even four men who cared enough to stay by my side no matter what, why wouldn't I ask them for help in doing the right thing?

All four of us slowly rose to standing. It felt oddly ceremonial, a *this is it* type of moment.

"Ready when you are, little fox." Hunter wrapped an arm around my shoulders and lowered a kiss to my forehead. I looked up at those golden eyes and remembered the first time I saw them—through the bars of a cage.

"I love you," I blurted out, my heart speeding up into overdrive like this could be the last chance I had to tell him. "You didn't have to come here or stay for this, but I'm so glad you're here with me."

"And I love you." He cupped my face and kissed me with all the heat and dominance of an alpha claiming his mate. "My place is by your side, no matter what."

We released each other, and I took a deep breath to cast an illusion over him. Again, I made him appear shorter and softened his physique to a normal dad-bod. I darkened his hair, eyes, and skin tone just enough to make him unremarkable before turning to Razvan.

"I know you love me, *steluța*," he chuckled, pulling me into a possessive embrace. "Don't act like we're saying goodbye. This is not the end of anything, okay? Besides our trip to America's swampy asshole."

He made me giggle, forcing me to put extra focus on Hunter's disguise so it would hold. His handsome face grinned at my reaction before giving me a long, slow, lingering kiss full of sensuality. He ensured I felt every part of that split tongue and took my breath away.

"I can't wait to taste you again when we're done being heroes," he smirked, running his thumb along my lower lip before he stepped back and proceeded to shift.

It felt like forever since I'd seen his dragon form in the flesh—all obsidian scales and fearsome horns, teeth and claws. I could only stare in awe as this creature the size of a large horse wrapped his tail around his feet and tucked his wings close to his body. He'd have a hell of a time leaving this suite without damaging anything.

Hunter's and Arjun's eyes widened in awe at the sight of him.

"Fuck me sideways, mate. All these years later and I still can't believe you're real," Arjun breathed.

"We're just waiting on you," I reminded the tiger shifter before reaching out to scratch Raz's scaly forehead. "Maybe you could fly out onto the balcony and meet us outside, dragon? Rather than going through the hotel."

Raz snorted two small plumes of gray smoke from his nostrils and jerked his large head up and down in a nod. *Might as well use these wings for something,* he thought, nuzzling against me.

With my dragon carefully following behind me, I went to open the sliding glass door to the balcony. If Raz crouched down and tucked his wings close, he could just squeeze through.

When I looked back at Arjun, a beautiful Bengal tiger returned my stare. He sat on his haunches, the tip of his tail flicking absently as he waited. Hunter stood patiently by the door, not even a flicker in his illusion.

I took a final deep breath to cast the next set of illusions—making Arjun and Raz invisible. Only a gust of wind told me that Raz left the building, and the sensation of a large furry head bumping my hand told me Arjun was close.

While looking as if we were alone, Hunter and I left the room for possibly the last time.

12

RAZVAN

Damn, it felt so good to fly again. And it was completely surreal flying over people's heads without them ever looking up. The gusts from my wings might as well had been another ocean breeze.

I knew it would take a minute for Mel, Arjun, and Hunter to leave the hotel, so I took my time soaring high. The sun felt wonderful on my scales, and the swells of hot air lifted me higher. The only thing better would be having Mel and Hunter on my back.

If we really did survive this, I'd have to bribe my *steluţa* into making me invisible more often. A half-dozen orgasms from my tongue should do the trick. I never realized how much I missed flying or my dragon form until I was in it. Around people I had to shift so sparingly, but with her abilities I might be able to more often.

I drifted lazily through the air until I spotted Hunter's disguise coming out of the hotel. I had to do a double-take at the woman he was with. Mel disguised herself as a shorter, curvy woman with blonde curls and an ample chest. She and

Hunter walked with some distance between them, indicating to me that Arjun walked there, unseen to those around him.

Did you do that just to torture me, steluța? I asked her, circling down closer above their heads. *I can see down your shirt and just want to run my tongue all over you.*

Behave, dragon, she teased back, lifting her eyes just slightly as she smiled. *Just thought I'd play around. I've never had a body like this.*

You could disguise yourself as a four-hundred pound man and I'd still want you, I answered. *Because I'd know it's really you under there.*

Romantic, she scoffed.

I have my moments.

She and Hunter continued down the street toward La Hacienda, careful to not let people walk between them. I followed just hovering above until we reached the alley behind the restaurant to carry out the second phase of our plan.

I still don't understand why I have to be a damn raccoon, Arjun whined.

Nobody will look twice at a trash panda, I reminded him.

A raccoon isn't even a cat, he complained. *At least you're still somewhat related to a dragon.*

An iguana eats only vegetables, can't fly or breathe fire, I retorted. *I think we're about even.*

Maybe it was inappropriate to be cracking jokes at a time like this, but who knew when we would laugh at each other again?

"Guys," Mel muttered, biting her lip to keep from laughing. "Get in here so I can focus."

I sensed Arjun following her, then landed softly to

ensure no nearby humans could feel the impact of my landing. To fit in the alley, I had to suck in my breath and hold my wings flush to my body. Thankfully, there was no one else in there or else they definitely would've felt my wings or possibly my scales.

Raz?

Right here, steluţa. I nuzzled against her side with my still-invisible head.

She turned toward me with a tense smile—even now she was trying to stay positive—and closed her eyes to cast the next set of illusions.

"Alright," she whispered. "Lead the way, Hunter."

Nothing changed from my perspective. I was still a dragon and Arjun was still a tiger, but to anyone else looking, Hunter and Mel were a couple of uniformed animal control officers carrying a surly raccoon and a large green iguana in metal cages.

You don't look that different to me, mate, I said to Arjun, now a fraction of his tiger's size as he peered through the bars of his cage with black, masked eyes and nimble, human-like hands.

Oh, shut your bloody mouth, lizard boy.

I resumed flying just overhead as the others walked the next few blocks to the hidden compound entrance. For me, that was the easiest way to not bump into humans and shatter the illusion. At about ten feet above their heads, my own head abruptly crashed into something solid and metal. And it made a shit ton of noise.

Fuck!

"Raz!" Mel hissed in surprise, stopping in her tracks and looking up at the seemingly empty sky above.

Don't look up! Arjun warned. *Nothing is there. You'll draw attention to yourself.*

Are you okay, dragon? Mel asked me with her mind.

Yeah. Fuck, sorry about the noise. There's an invisible barrier here. Must be part of the compound. The entrance is just at the next block, so it makes sense.

Are we good to keep going? Uncertainty crept into Mel's mental voice.

Yes, a few humans looked around, but they're back to minding their own business. I'm going to walk behind you guys now.

I landed softly on the sidewalk behind Mel and Hunter's heels, lowering my snout to sniff the ground. Like Arjun that first time, I could smell that many shifters walked this same path. Some scents were old, others as recent as a few hours ago. And just after the next intersection, the scent just disappeared.

Here we are, I said. *Now, do exactly as I say, steluţa. Turn straight to your left and walk ten steps.* She did as instructed, walking toward a fence between two buildings. The fence was a typical chain-link over wooden slats that didn't allow anyone to see to the other side. There were no gaps in it either, to the untrained eye.

Good. Now left again, three steps. Now right, five steps. Lean forward and you'll see a gap in the fence. Go through it.

She did so and paused. *I can barely squeeze through it. Will you be able to get in, dragon?*

Yes, the small doorway is just an illusion, too. It's actually huge, like a warehouse door. You'll see.

In the next moment, she was gone.

After double-checking to make sure no humans would be passing by, I walked through the same opening. In the next moment, Mel, Hunter, Arjun, and I stood at the entrance to a large, square building made of concrete and metal. Aside from the two double doors in front of us, the building had no windows.

It's all you now, dove, Arjun told her gently. *We're all here with you.*

Just tell her you're in love with her already... I wanted to say to him, but kept the thought to myself. I was quite certain Mel could not only hear us, but that it was her Speak ability that allowed us to talk amongst each other.

After a moment of pause, she stepped confidently up to the door and pushed it open. Following her, Hunter held it open long enough for Arjun and I to slip through.

You good, wolf? I gave Hunter a soft nudge on his shoulder, noticing he'd been silent since we left the hotel. He nodded sharply, but the tension in his body was palpable.

The hallway seemed to stretch on endlessly like a long, metallic tube with only fluorescent lights and the occasional unmarked door on either side. We didn't pass by anyone else, but I was ready, the fire swelling in my chest in preparation for any threat.

You know where you're going? Arjun asked Mel after a minute or so.

I think so, she answered. Her confident stride didn't betray any uncertainty, and Hunter simply followed her lead.

The hallway ended by splitting in two opposite directions. Mel turned to the left without any hesitation, nearly running headfirst into a woman wearing a white lab coat.

"Oh, I'm sorry!" Mel forced out a dry laugh while I hurriedly glued myself to the opposite wall.

"It's alright. Ugh, more vermin species, huh?" The woman shook her head at the caged raccoon and iguana. "I feel bad for you guys having to go out and catch these. It's like, why bother? I keep telling him we need the exotic animals, not another pest."

"I know," Mel sighed, doing a convincing job of commiserating with the woman. "Just doin' what we're told, ya know?"

"I hear ya." The woman rolled her eyes before continuing down the hallway. "Hope you land a big one soon! I'm dying for another dolphin, personally."

"I'll keep that in mind," Mel called after her, then visibly shuddered when she turned out of sight. Hunter approached her like he was going to put his arm around her in comfort, but she picked up the iguana cage and resumed marching down the hallway.

"Lhozen is yours, Arjun. But that bitch is mine," she growled through gritted teeth.

On any other day, I would have pinned her against the wall and taken her sweet little body right then and there. I loved when my woman got aggressive. Seeing that fire in her got me hard, unlike anything else. But we had to survive this first.

The right wall of this new hallway soon opened up to a bay of windows looking over a large, open room below. And what I saw, I'll never be able to unsee again.

Rows of cages crammed up against each other and stacked precariously high on top of each other. Each one held some different kind of creature. I didn't want to say animal, because many were partially shifted, obviously stuck between forms from the drugs they'd been given. These poor shifters were beyond freakish, if even nightmarish in appearance. Some of them looked deformed due to injury or trauma, or possibly because they were simply the victims of sick experiments.

Melody, Arjun barked, his mental voice ringing like a bell in my head. *You're losing the illusions. Stay focused. Shut them out.*

"How can they...?" Mel whispered, staring through the glass as her eyes welled up with tears. "Oh my God. How can they do this? They're *people.*"

A glance down at the floor sent my pulse into over-drive. I could see my own black scales and claws turning opaque, while the iguana and cage in Hunter's hand was fading into nothingness.

Steluța, I'm going to be seen, I told her. *You have to focus, or we have to leave.*

"We can't leave them." A choked sob escaped her throat as she raised a hand to the glass. On the other side of her, orange and black stripes became more clear and solid with each passing second.

"Mel! Little fox!" Hunter, now at his normal height with his skin slowly becoming paler, grabbed her arm and turned her around to face him. He clapped his hands to her cheeks, forcing her to look at him. "Mel, if we're seen, we're done for. We *need* you to hold up the illusions—"

The sound of clanking metal overpowered his words. Like in some kind of sci-fi movie, a heavy door slid out of the wall from the direction we just came from, cutting off our way out. Up ahead, a similar door cut off the opposite end of the hallway.

Just like that, we were fucking trapped.

"I daresay, the ones with the bleeding hearts are always the most gullible," a clipped English accent announced cheerily.

We all turned to see the same woman we passed in the hallway, smiling as she casually leaned against one of the many unmarked doors.

"Lhozen," Arjun voiced, barely above a whisper. I didn't even notice he had shifted to human.

"I'm sorry for not saying a proper hello, my dear stepson," the woman chuckled in the same English accent, now with a man's voice. "I thought I'd try a new look."

Her form shifted before our eyes, stretching up to the height of a man in his fifties, with salt and pepper hair, blue eyes, and an expensive tailored suit on a slim build. I recognized him immediately. He spoke fluent Romanian to my parents right before he purchased me, then personally shoved swords down my throat until I learned to take them without flinching.

My jaws opened, ready to spill the fire that raged inside me at this man for years. I knew he was Arjun's to kill, but none of that mattered now. We would either die or never leave this compound if he wasn't eliminated right the fuck now.

Lhozen held up a hand in front of my snout, palm open and completely unafraid.

"Not so fast, Razvan. Don't you feel like you're getting sleepy?"

What the...

"Why don't you take a nap?"

The last thing I saw was my reflection in his shoes, polished to a high shine before my head hit the floor.

13

CONNOR

The drive to Georgia was mostly silent. I didn't try to force small talk between Jeanie or the young ones. I was still a stranger to them and had no desire to make them more uncomfortable.

Whenever Jeanie requested stopping for bathroom breaks or food, I agreed without question. It was only in the last hour to the FDR center she started talking to me unprompted.

"How did you meet Mel?" she began.

My knuckles whitened on the steering wheel as my hands clenched at the memory. I never imagined I would think of Syko again.

"A guy was trying to take advantage of her," I answered. "It was her first time onstage at a carnival, which made it even worse. Poor thing was like a deer in headlights up there. At her first chance, she bolted."

"And let me guess. You were her knight in shining armor," Jeanie remarked sarcastically.

"Not exactly," I laughed. "You'll see I'm not that type

at all. But she slipped and fell in the mud, then threw up all over herself. Don't let her know I told you that."

"Wow. That must've been sexy."

"Love at first sight," I cracked. "But no, actually, I did feel bad. So I gave her water and let her use my trailer to shower in, while I stayed far away. I tried to keep staying far away, but she never left me alone."

"So when did y'all fall in love?"

"Hm, for me?" I took a moment to think about when exactly it happened. It was crystal clear to me, but I felt a little unsure about spilling that to Jeanie.

"I guess it was when I had a bad PTSD episode." Fuck it, why not? She was Mel's family, and would figure it out when she saw the FDR center, anyway. "Mine gets triggered by noises like gunshots or fireworks sometimes. Mel stayed with me the whole time and just calmed me down. No one had really done that for me before, so that was when I knew she was special."

"PTSD?" Jeanie asked.

I nodded and reached down to lift up my pant leg.

"Holy shit," she breathed.

"It's not my place to tell you what to do with your life, but I don't recommend joining the military," I snorted. "It worked out alright for me, but I wouldn't wish the hell I went through on anybody else."

Except maybe Lhozen.

My heart tightened uncomfortably in my chest. *Lord almighty, please keep my babe and those three knuckleheads safe.* I wished more than anything I could hear her voice in my head like they could. Only two days away from her and I was already fighting every instinct to turn this bitch around and run to be at her side.

Maybe Jeanie was onto something, and I was more of a knight in shining armor than I cared to admit. Or maybe falling in love with Mel made me that way.

"So Mel's a circus performer or whatever now?" Jeanie said. "That's why she couldn't come get us herself?"

"She's a ringmistress, yes," I said evenly. "But that's not why she couldn't come."

"Y'all said it was because of work. Like, I get that she's trying to provide for us. Be the mother we never had or whatever, but we were about to be homeless. The kids miss her more than anything. They don't even want any birthday presents, they just want to see her. And she couldn't get out of work to see them?"

"I get it, Jeanie. I really do. But it's not as simple as that. You don't know the whole story."

"So what is the whole story?"

"Mel should be the one to tell you."

With a scoff and an eye roll, Jeanie crossed her arms and turned to look out the passenger-side window, in typical teenage fashion. I was her age not too long ago, so it didn't bother me much. We drove on in silence until we came onto the grounds of the FDR Center.

Home sweet home. But it wouldn't feel like home until I had my woman back in my arms.

"You live *here?*" Jeanie forgot she was pissed at me as she pressed her nose to the glass, taking in the colorful flower beds and topiaries that flanked the driveway to the main building.

"Not in there," I chuckled, following the road around the main building as I waved to one of the landscapers. "But we live on campus. You'll see."

"What is this place?"

"It's a non-profit center for disabled veterans," I answered. "I'm pretty certain your sister and this place have both saved my life. They custom-made these legs for me." I knocked on my metallic left shin as the road turned to gravel and the landscape grew wilder.

Jeanie's knuckles whitened as she gripped the armrests of her seat. I could guess what she was thinking about this guy driving her and three small children deeper into the woods. I couldn't think of how to reassure her. Like she said earlier, I could lie about anything. I just had to wait it out and prove that we weren't abusive or axe murderers.

The plantation house soon came into view, but that wasn't what captured the attention of Joey and Bella as they pressed their faces to the windows.

"Puppies!" Bella squealed. "I see puppies! Two of them!"

"What? I want one!" Riley demanded, squeezing between her siblings to see.

"Hey! Sit down and buckle up, the car's still moving!" Jeanie barked at them.

I rubbed my jaw as we pulled up to the house, where Colt, Gabe, and Miriam relaxed on the front porch while the pups ran wild. I forgot that they might be even more rambunctious without their father around. It seemed I'd have to explain some things to Jeanie before Mel got back.

"I want you to know something," I said, slowing the RV to a halt and turning to grab Jeanie's hand before shutting the engine off.

"What?" She looked surprised, even put off a little by the contact, but she didn't pull away.

"You're safe here," I told her. "The kids are safe here. You're not in danger. You're going to see some shit that's weird, but I promise you no one will hurt you or the young ones anymore."

She gave a strange, squinty-eyed look with a tilt of her head. "What the hell are you talking about?"

"I know me saying that just set your alarm bells ringing," I patted her hand before letting go and standing up. "But you can trust me and anyone here. Just remember what I said."

"Oh. Kay..." She got out of her own seat and marched back to gather the kids. "Come on guys, hold hands. I know you want to meet the puppies, but Connor's going out first."

Here goes nothin'.

I popped open the door, wincing slightly at the impact of the ground. I definitely over-wore my legs on this road trip and needed a few days without them, or I'd never hear the end of it from my doctors and Mel.

"Connor!" Colt and Miriam approached the RV, arms around each other in an affectionate embrace. "We didn't expect to see you back so soon. Where is everyone?"

"Still in Florida," I answered before lowering my voice. "I had to get Mel's siblings out of a bad situation. They're all completely human. As in, they have no idea about any of this."

"Leave it to me," Miriam winked before releasing her wolf shifter's arm and looked past me to Jeanie wrangling the young ones. "Hi! You must be Mel's family."

"Uh, yeah. Hi." Jeanie's eyes darted around as she pulled Bella and Joey close, securing Riley on her hip.

"I'm Miriam, and this is Colt. You'll meet the others later. Can I help y'all bring in anything? Are you hungry?"

"Uh, I think we're okay—"

"Here, let me get that for you." Before Jeanie could protest, Miriam marched over and took the backpack sliding off her shoulder. "I can show you the bedrooms and you can pick which ones you and the kids would like."

"Uh, thanks. How many people live here?" Jeanie looked up at the two-story plantation house, as if noticing it for the first time.

"Mel, her guys, and the pups make seven," Miriam said. "I live with Colt and Gabe in a cabin a bit deeper in the woods. We're just house-sitting and watching the kids while Mel and everyone's away."

"Kids? What kids?"

"Hunter's pups." Colt cocked his head toward the lawn where Roo and Rinna chased each other and wrestled playfully.

Jeanie forced an awkward chuckle while Miriam and I glared at Colt. "He loves his puppies enough to call them his kids. That's cute."

Just then, the pups took notice of me and ran over as fast as their four legs could carry them, mouths open in wide smiles and tongues lolling out.

"Shit," I muttered under my breath, but forced a smile as they ran closer.

Just as I feared, they began shifting to human mid-run.

"Mr. Connor, you're back!" Roo called as soon as he had a human mouth.

"Holy fuck! What the—" Jeanie clapped a hand over her mouth before pulling Bella and Joey close to her side.

"Jesus," I muttered, pulling off my shirt and tossing it to Colt to cover Hunter's now-naked children clamoring around us. "Hey," I placed a hand on Jeanie's shoulder, "remember what I told you, okay? You're not in danger here. They're just kids... who also happen to be wolf pups."

"What the fuck is going on?" she stared at me wide-eyed. "What are they? What are *you?* How the hell did my sister get involved with all of you?"

"I'll tell you everything," I promised her. "As for me, I'm nothing special. Just a surly ex-Marine missing a few limbs and brain cells."

"Hi."

At our feet, Bella walked right up to Rinna, who now wore my shirt around her like a huge tent of a dress. "Are you a girl or a puppy?"

"I'm both!" Rinna declared proudly. "My daddy is a man and a wolf. My name's Rinna. That's my brother, Roo."

"I'm Bella," Mel's younger sister giggled. "Can I call you Rella?"

"Sure. Do you want to play tag?"

"Okay!"

"Rinna," Colt crouched low to the ground to talk to his niece. He spoke in a low, gentle voice about ground rules like wearing clothes and staying in human form when playing with humans. She listened with rapt attention and nodded, clearly excited to play with someone other than her brother.

"Wait, hold on," Jeanie's arm shot out and yanked Bella back to her side. "No one is playing with anyone until someone explains this stuff."

"Come inside, Jeanie," Miriam suggested gently, holding her arm out. "I'm a regular human like Connor. I can't shift either. We'll explain everything and answer any questions you have, I promise."

Jeanie's wide, panicked eyes darted from me to Miriam as she struggled to make her choice. I understood how difficult it was for her to trust and knew we shouldn't push her. She came all this way with me having no idea what she was getting into, and had certainly not expected anything like this.

"Okay," she said finally.

With that, we all turned to head into the house. I gave Miriam a quick glance and she returned it with a small nod and smile. It might take some time, but we were making progress. For all we knew, Mel and the others would come home to find her siblings completely at ease and feeling at home with shifters in their new family

MELODY

My eyelids felt like they weighed ten pounds each as I fought to open them. My throat felt like a desert and my head swam in a fog, but I didn't feel pain anywhere.

When I finally forced my eyes open, my body wanted to tense up, but it wouldn't obey. My limbs felt heavy and too relaxed. In fact, whatever I was lying on was soft and comfortable, like the loveseat at home where I would happily curl up for a nap.

I looked up at a dark ceiling with a simple chandelier, casting warm yellow light throughout the room. The walls were dark wood paneling lined with bookshelves. An antique wooden desk sat in the corner, its feet rested on a large area rug with an intricate design. When I pressed myself up to sitting, I realized I had been reclining on a loveseat. It felt plush, soft, and expensive.

Something was all wrong about this. I was in someone's cozy office, not a prison for shifters.

"Ah, good. You're awake."

All too slowly, my head turned to the voice. The man I now knew was Lhozen smiled cheerfully back at me.

"You must be parched, dear," he said in a charming English accent. "There's a glass of water on the table next to you." At my suspicious look, he added, "Oh, there's no need for that look. I haven't put anything in it. Why would I want to harm the next most powerful shaman besides me?"

"The guys," I croaked through my dry mouth. "My shifters. Where are they?"

"With the others," he said dismissively, walking over to the desk to rifle through some papers. "Drink up, Melody. Are you hungry as well? My kitchen can prepare anything you'd like. We have much to discuss and I want you in top shape, love."

"The others?" I demanded, my voice growing stronger as if everything he said after that never even registered. "You mean caged and brutalized? Disfigured and tortured? What makes you think I would ever want to cooperate with you?"

Lhozen let out a patronizing sigh. "What you saw through the window, dear, was merely another illusion." He waved a hand theatrically in front of his face. "But I can certainly make it a reality should you decide not to cooperate." The charm never left his smile, but I saw something dark and sinister in his eyes for the first time.

So the monstrosities I saw weren't real? That was a relief, albeit a tiny one. The visions in my head and what I saw through Julian's eyes weren't much better though.

"What do you want from me?" I demanded. "What's the point of this place and why do you even need my cooperation?"

"Because you are like a daughter to me, Melody." The charming grin grew wider. "The young protege I've always wanted but could never find. Miriam showed promise, but unfortunately she was not very intelligent or strong enough."

"What?" None of what he said made sense. I never met this man before in my life, and even what he said about Miriam puzzled me. She had future Sight, how could she not be smart or strong enough? But I kept my face blank and tried to absorb whatever information he might tell me. Who knew if it would be useful to getting the guys out of here.

"You don't remember me, do you?" He looked disappointed and clicked his tongue at me. "Here, maybe this will jog your memory."

He waved a hand, now encased in a white glove, over his head, where he now wore a silky black top hat. I flinched when he reached that hand out to touch me, but his gloved fingers only gently grazed the shell of my ear. Just as quickly, he pulled his hand away, holding a coin between two fingers.

The realization made my heart drop into my stomach.

No way. Please no. It can't be.

"You've made me proud, Melody. You took the gift of my powers better than anyone else I've ever seen." He flipped the coin in the air and it landed next to me on the sofa, the crossed daggers shining up at me. They reminded me of Razvan and my gut twisted into a series of tight knots at my confusion and dread.

"Why?" I squeaked out. I didn't even know what I was asking. Why me? Why was he doing this to shifters, including his own stepson? What sick, twisted purpose did he have in mind for me?

"Oh, the decision was easy," he said lightheartedly, the gloves and top hat illusions now gone. "Even as a seven-year-old child, you had magic in you. I saw it in the way you calmed your sister down and distracted her from your horrible beast of a mother."

"Don't," I threw up a hand, my temper going from zero to sixty within seconds, "say one goddamn word about my mother. You raised Arjun like your own son and then did *this* to him? He couldn't fucking walk, because he'd been in tiger form for so long. He trusted you! And the whole time, you're treating shifters like lab mice?!"

"My dear, you are young," he said with that same dismissive, patronizing tone. "You're not seeing the big picture, and I'll forgive your ignorance for now. You still need training to build your powers and—"

"Forget it." I crossed my arms defiantly. If he was going to treat me like a child, I was happy to act like one. "I don't give a shit if you gave me my abilities, I'm not training under you."

"You may want to rethink that, Melody." His voice took on the undertone of a threat. "Believe it or not, I take no pleasure in the pain of others. But if you do not go along with my plan that I have so carefully constructed over the past eight years, there will be consequences."

When I said nothing, keeping my arms crossed, he gave a curt nod and said, "Very well." He snapped his fingers, then two men in dark green, military-style fatigues marched through the door and took hold of my arms.

"What the—! Let me go!"

"I warned you, Melody." Lhozen almost sounded apologetic. "But perhaps it's best that you learn what I'm capable of. Oh, Renson?"

"Yes, sir?" asked one of the men holding my arm.

"Give her lovers metamorparfizan before you let her have some time with them. Make sure she sees."

"Yes, sir."

The guards began dragging me out of the room, not roughly, but firm-handed enough that I couldn't get my feet under me.

"Jesus, stop it. I can walk on my own," I protested.

They humored me, slowing enough for me to regain my footing and walk between them. Each man's fingers dug into my biceps like vice grips, which I tried to ignore. It sparked a memory of my mom leaving bruises when she grabbed my arms and shook me to scream in my face, but I swallowed it down. I had to keep it together for the guys.

The hallway outside of Lhozen's office looked exactly the same as the one we stood in before getting caught. I couldn't tell if it was the same anymore since he apparently illusioned the shit out of this place.

I craned my neck to the right side, looking through the large bay window to the open area down below. The same cages still lined the floors and stood stacked on top of each other, but everyone was in animal form as far as I could see. No partially-shifted or mutated freaks.

A chill ran through me. How did Lhozen know seeing shifters like that would throw off my focus? Did he just assume I'd be freaked out by that, as most people would be? I had a nagging feeling he knew more than he let on.

Aside from the compound humans talking in low voices and the hum of machinery, I also realized no one was screaming. Bears, owls, coyotes, bobcats, foxes, and more all sat quietly in their cages. Their blank, glassy-eyed stares made me wonder if they were sedated.

My guards led me down a flight of stairs to the cage area. A few people in lab coats worked on computers at a metal table in the center of the room. Around the perimeter of the room, I noticed heavy metal doors with small square windows in them. Squinting through, I could see some people in hazmat suits through those doors, but the windows were too small to see what they were doing.

"Hold her," one of my guards said to the other. One man now crushed both of my biceps in an uncomfortably tight grip.

My eyes darted around the room as he held me, trying to take in as much information as possible. Were there any exits to the outside in this room? Could I cast any illusions in here to distract the humans and get the shifters out?

"Don't even think about it, missy," my guard sneered as if reading my mind. "Lhozen will know the second you try to fool us."

My teeth gritted in my jaw. Come on, Mel, think. Lhozen isn't all-powerful. He isn't a god. There's got to be a way.

"Got 'em," my other guard called from behind us. "Bring 'em out."

The one holding me spun us around just as a large cage began moving toward us on some kind of pulley system. It was in a dark, back corner of the room, slowly coming out toward the center on a track in the floor. This cage was huge—big enough to hold a dinosaur or a—

"Raz!" I cried out, trying to bolt toward the cage, but the guard held me still.

Steluţa!

My dragon barely had room to turn around in his barred prison. His wings pressed against the top, unable to stretch out fully. The moment he saw me, he let out a terrifying roar and reached for me, stretching one clawed hand through the bars and nearly swiping the lab coat off a nearby human.

Underneath Raz was an unmoving mass of white fur. My dragon stood protectively over the white wolf and somehow, the sight of Hunter's still form allowed to me to break free of my guard's hold.

"No, no, Hunter!" I pressed my face between the bars, grabbing hold of Raz's claw as it caressed over my face. "Hunter, get up!"

He's alive, but he bit someone, so they gave him a huge dose of sedative. I can barely feel his heart.

"Fuck..." I looked up at my dragon's face, covered in obsidian scales and horns, but those same steel-gray eyes were so human as they looked back at me.

Raz, can you breathe fire? If you torch someone and get them to panic, they'll be distracted and I can—

I can't, steluța, he told me mournfully. They stuck me with so many injections when Lhozen knocked me out. Every time I try, I feel like I'm choking.

I leaned my forehead against his clawed hand, despair swallowing me up like quicksand. I couldn't even bring myself to cry, so I just watched Hunter breathing weakly.

What about Arjun? I asked Raz. Have you seen him?

No, my love. He's not in a cage. I don't know where they're keeping him.

"Alright, time to move this sweet reunion along," someone muttered behind me.

Before I could react, something shot past my head and

struck Razvan's arm. He let me go with a scream and began thrashing wildly against the cage bars.

"What did you do?!" I cried, trying to reach for him, but someone grabbed my arms again.

I watched helplessly as my dragon roared in pain while he spasmed, hitting his head against the bars and nearly stepping on Hunter's lifeless form as he seemed to lose control of his body. Someone else was screaming too, and only when a hand clapped roughly over my mouth did I realize it was me.

After what felt like hours, but had to be only seconds, I noticed Raz's form was shrinking. His tail and wings disappeared into his body, his arms and legs rearranged to be roughly human in shape. His head shrank down to human size, but he still kept a layer of black scales over his skin. His horns and dragon teeth remained, giving him a demon-like appearance.

And there the forced shifting stopped.

"Still wanna kiss your lizard boy?" a mocking voice asked. "Go ahead."

The door to the cage opened, and in the next moment, I was flying through. The tears fell freely now as I wrapped my arms around Raz's neck, sobbing uncontrollably into his shoulder. He cradled my back, gently stroking my hair as if it was his duty to comfort me after what had just been done to him.

My hand drifted down his scaled arm until it met the injected needle they just shot at him. I yanked on it with all my strength, making him flinch and grunt with pain. What I pulled from his arm was at least four inches long and thicker than a toothpick.

"Thyrrr." Raz attempted to speak, but his jaws were

still too dragon-like. A soft chuckle floated around us from the observing humans, and it made my blood boil. They did this to humiliate him.

They strengthened their needles since I was last captured, he told me sadly. Now they can penetrate my dragon hide instead of sticking me when I'm human.

"Dragon, I'm so sorry." I curled up against him, laying my head on the black scales of his chest as sobs wracked my body. "I'll get you out of here. I don't know how, but I will."

A mocking, "*Awww,*" rose up from around us. My body immediately tensed and I moved to lift my head, but Raz pulled me tightly against him, a clawed hand cupping my face.

Do not try to bargain with Lhozen, he said. Don't believe his lies. If he offers to set us free in order to keep you, it's a trick. Everything he is, is an illusion, steluţa. Don't make deals. Don't trust him.

A cocking sound made us both look up.

"No, don't!" I moved to cover Hunter with my own body, but wasn't fast enough. The fired injection stuck him on his flank.

Grab him, Raz ordered. He's going to seize like I did. Make sure he doesn't hurt himself.

Together, we held Hunter's body as still as we possibly could while the onlooking humans chuckled and made their insulting comments. We ignored them, but I took note of everyone, making sure to remember every face and name tag.

I held our wolf's head in my lap while Raz held down his spasming arms and legs. There must have been some amount of adrenaline in the forced-shifting drug, because Hunter's golden eyes shot open, wide, and dilated.

"I'm sorry, my love," I leaned down and kissed his forehead as he grunted and struggled through the forced shifting. "I'm so, so sorry."

Hey, handsome, Raz said, lacing his clawed, scaly fingers through Hunter's human-like paw. *You look just like when I first saw you.*

"Rarrz?" Hunter blinked and began looking around—first at me and Raz, then down at his body stuck between wolf and human.

I didn't give a fuck that humans were looking at us like animals in a zoo and laughing. All I wanted was to stay with my wolf and dragon, but someone grabbed my arms and dragged me, kicking and screaming, out of the cage.

15

MELODY

"You can take me back to Lhozen," I murmured in a daze, my feet no longer working like they were supposed to. My guards actually had to drag me across the floor this time. "I'll do whatever he wants me to do, just don't hurt them anymore."

"Not so fast, sweetie," one of them chuckled. "We have one more for you to visit."

Arjun. Oh god, Arjun.

I tried twisting my head around to look back at Raz and Hunter, but my left guard jerked on my arm. Pain shot through my shoulder as I yelped. The asshole had nearly yanked my arm out of my socket.

At least my dragon and my wolf had each other. I found the smallest possible comfort in that fact.

My guards dragged me to one of the metal doors in the walls with tiny square windows. One of them waved a card over a panel next to the door, which beeped and a small green light turned on. The door slid open and there was my tiger.

Human and naked, his back pressed against the rear wall of the tiny room, no bigger than a walk-in closet. His ocean-colored eyes, wide with fear, didn't notice me. Right away, I knew why.

Hoops of fire lined the floor like some kind of hopscotch layout from Hell. The flames jumped and crackled, sending sparks in the air. But something wasn't right.

My guards shoved me before I could process and think. With a scream, I teetered forward, heat enveloping my body as I swung wildly in midair for something to hold on to. Bracing myself for the pain of being burned alive, I crashed to the floor on my hands and knees.

"Melody!" Arjun screamed.

Immediately I rolled, instinct taking over. I must've rolled five or six times across the floor before it hit me: I wasn't on fire.

I stopped, my heart going a mile a minute, and held my hands out in front of my face.

Another fucking illusion. *I'm not really burning.*

My lips moved rapidly as I repeated the mantra over and over, trying to calm the panic response in my body. *This fire isn't real. I'm not burning.*

When I sat up, Arjun's head was in his hands. His fingers gripped so tight in his thick black hair, I was afraid he'd pull it out.

"Arjun?" I scooted across the floor and touched his bare shoulder. Only then did I realize he was trembling.

"Arjun, it's okay." I kissed his hair and his brow as my hands slid over his, gently trying to unlock his fingers. "The fire isn't real."

"Nothing is okay," he muttered. "None of this is fucking okay."

Any determination I had to get us out withered away into nothing at that moment. I collapsed into sobs right there, my forehead pressed to his and my fingers locked in his.

"I'm so sorry." How many times had I said that already? I felt like the most pathetic idiot on the planet. "You were right. I should have listened to you. Everything we planned, everything you taught me. None of it mattered. Now he's hurting all of you and this is all my fault."

At some point, his hands wrapped around me. He held me against his chest and, for once, I didn't care that he was naked. I kissed his neck, his collarbone, his mouth. I didn't know what else to do, how else to convey how much I regretted putting him and the others in this place.

"We should have gone home," I whispered mournfully. "We'd be with my siblings, with the pups, with Connor, at our beautiful house. Oh god, at least Connor isn't here."

He held me wordlessly for a few moments, fingers grazing along the nape of my neck. I couldn't tell if it was absent minded or if he was intentionally touching me in one of my most sensitive areas.

"If we did that, would things have gone back to the way before?" he asked with surprising nonchalance.

I paused to let a few ragged breaths, and sobs escape my chest. "What do you mean?"

"I mean this." He cupped my chin roughly and kissed me. Those lips and tongue seemed to take my breath away and give me new life at the same time. My world spun, and I was soaring. My arms ached from my guards manhandling me. My heart was shattered at how my men and every shifter in here were being treated. Maybe that was why Arjun tasted so fucking good and I couldn't stop.

"Would I have you like this?" he murmured gruffly, teeth trailing down my jaw to my neck, "if we weren't trapped in a fucking metal box? Would you be here, soothing me away from what I fear most, if we weren't close to death?"

"Arjun..." His hand closed over my breast, tugging on my nipple through my clothes as his mouth sent nerve endings tingling through my neck. Oh god, was I getting wet? My brain spun with confusion. How could I be getting turned on right now, of all times?

"Answer me," he growled, though I wasn't sure he really wanted an answer. "Do I want you so fucking bad because I might not be alive tomorrow? Do you feel so good because I'll never get another chance to touch you again?"

"I don't know, Arjun." Tears escaped my eyes, but he raised his face to kiss them away, his mouth soon capturing mine again. My lips felt delightfully bruised when he pulled away softly.

"Or is it because you're meant to be my mate?" he whispered. "Like my tiger believed the moment I first heard your voice in my head, and I've been too fucking stubborn this whole time to admit it?"

"I think... the second one."

He pulled away, his eyes meeting mine, and blinked. "Well, *that* was anticlimactic."

I let out a dry laugh. I actually *laughed* despite this horrible situation we were in. How adorably cliche to admit one's feelings right before almost certain death?

"I knew I wanted you before all this happened," I whispered. "But it probably took a while for me to admit it, too."

The handsome tiger inhaled deeply, caressing my nape again in a way that made me forget everything outside of his touch.

"Well, aside from our delightful parents, there's another thing we have in common."

A smirk played on his lips, and I found myself smiling back. My pulse thrummed in my veins, but not from fear or adrenaline this time. For a moment, it was that euphoric feeling upon first pouring your heart out—somewhere between awkward embarrassment and uncontrollable happiness. Just for the briefest moment in time, it was just us basking in that feeling.

Then someone banged on the metal door, followed by yelling and whistles from the other side. Of course, they were watching us like a spectator sport too.

"I don't suppose you want our first time together in front of an audience," Arjun mused.

"And if it's our last time, too?" I wrapped my hands around his neck. "Let them watch. I don't care."

My lips descended on his, never separating, as I shifted my legs around to straddle him. He let out a hot moan as I leaned into his erection. If his cock was the last one I ever rode, I'd die a happy woman. My fingers drifted down his taut chest and abs to wrap around the base. He was deliciously thick and curved upward slightly when hard. By the way he had touched me already, I knew he wasn't a selfish lover.

"Mel, dove." His lips broke away from mine, sucking between his teeth as his hand stopped my upward strokes on his shaft.

"What's wrong?" Goddamn, I was already panting. Was I ready to die so quickly?

"I'm not making love to you here in a filthy prison cell." His heated gaze kept an air of playfulness but also determination. "If you want this, you've got to get us out of here, love."

"What? You're not seriously rejecting me again?"

"I am, but not because I want to," he said huskily. "I don't want some rushed half-assed fuck. I want to savor every piece of you after all this is over."

I blinked at him. "But you just said—"

"I know what I said, love." He pushed my hair away from my face, cupping my cheek as he kissed me deeply again. "The odds are still against us. But if anyone can beat them, Melody, it's you."

"How?" The noise outside our cell rose, and I knew our time was limited. Our captors weren't getting the show they originally wanted, and now they were bored. "Arjun, if anyone can tell me how, I know it's you."

"No, my beautiful dove. It's all you," he said quickly as we heard the telltale beep of someone scanning their card to open the door. "You're not just a shaman, you're a ring-mistress. Command the stage. You own it."

His gaze bore into mine as the guards' brutal hands dug into my arms to drag me away. I didn't struggle against them, but my mind raced at his words. I knew he was speaking in a metaphor, but why? And what was he trying to tell me?

"Now you can go to Lhozen," my left guard sneered at me. "He'll have a whole army of half-animal freaks to fuck you. Isn't that what you like?"

I would have spit at him, maybe tossed out a *fuck you*

and gotten my arm dislocated as a result. And it would have been worth it. But I had more important things to worry about now.

I had to figure out what the hell Arjun meant. And fast.

16

CONNOR

"So what you're actually telling me is, there are people who can turn into animals?"

"Yes," Miriam answered Jeanie's question calmly. "And your sister Mel is like me, a shaman. We have a close connection with shifters. We sense them and communicate with them in ways normal humans can't."

"But most humans are like you and me," I told Mel's wide-eyed sister. "We're stuck with the bodies we have and we're as magical as a can of beans."

"I know it's a lot to take in," Miriam added to Jeanie's stunned silence, keeping her voice warm and soothing. "But you get used to it after spending more time with them. And you realize they're just people like anyone else." She affectionately poked Colt in the ribs, who grabbed her finger and pretended to bite it.

"It's so weird, it's like... I can't explain it," Jeanie shook her head. "Like, I am shocked and I'm not all at the same time. Like I always *knew* there was magic and other beings like y'all existed, but I forgot I knew that. I guess I figured it was my imagination just trying to escape the bullshit that was part of my everyday life."

"Both you and Mel were like that, I bet," I said, trying to ignore the ache in my chest. Goddamn, I missed her like crazy.

"Yeah," Jeanie nodded, her eyes lighting up. "When everyone passed out, we used to play pretend all the time. Mel was always saving dragons and unicorns from evil. She talked to them like they were people."

I couldn't suppress the grin spreading across my mouth. *Just wait until you meet Razvan,* I thought.

"Dragons are totally real," Colt chimed in. "Your sister has one of those, too. Never seen a unicorn, but I wouldn't rule it out."

"Raz might be the last one," I added. "Unless others with the dormant shift pop up. His family thought they were humans for centuries."

"Jesus, *dragons?*" Jeanie slapped a palm to her forehead.

"Do you want to lie down?" Miriam offered. "It's been a long trek and I know this is information overload."

"Yeah, that might be a good idea, but," she hesitated. "Who's gonna watch the kids?"

"We will. Don't worry about it." Miriam stood, hovering over Jeanie like a mother hen as she prepared to lead her to a bedroom.

"I'm not tired. Can I play tag?" Bella asked, sliding off of her own seat.

"It's really okay," I said in response to Jeanie's worried look. "All the open space around the house is ours. We'll keep an eye on them, promise."

Jeanie finally resigned with a nod, her eyelids drooping

like she hadn't slept in days, and got up to follow Miriam. Once the two of them ascended the stairs, Rinna grabbed Bella's hands and squealed excitedly.

"You guys know the rules." Colt leaned down to playfully tap Rinna's nose. "Human form only and don't go past the treeline. We'll be watching. I'll drag you back by your scruff if I have to."

"Humans don't have scruffs, Uncle Colt," Rinna giggled.

"You will after I'm done with you," he teased, tickling her sides and blowing raspberries on her cheeks until she ran away laughing. With the kids outside and the ladies gone, it was just me and Hunter's dark-haired brother left in the room.

"Coming around to humans, are ya, Colt?" The question was casual enough, but I wanted him to know I hadn't stopped keeping an eye on him and Gabe. This was still *my* house, and Jeanie was *my* mate's sister. I let the brothers know when they first showed up they had only one chance to disrespect us and they'd be gone, regardless of how they felt about humans.

"I've never been against humans as a whole, Connor," he answered. "Do I have some resentment? Some grudges toward certain individuals? Yes, of course. But I'm not a puritan. I've never been against human and shifter pairings, or even interspecies-shifter pairing. That puritanical way of thinking is dying out. At least, the few remaining wolf packs need to see that if they want to survive."

"What about Gabe?" I asked. "Haven't even seen his face since we got back."

"Gabe is... conflicted," he sighed. "Typical youngster, always having an identity crisis. He's completely in love with Miriam, but hates himself for it. He's afraid of wanting to be okay with how the world is changing, so he's spent the last couple days in wolf form trying to ignore that it's happening."

"How is the world changing?"

He lifted an eyebrow. "Don't you know?"

"I want to hear it from your perspective." I leaned back in my wheelchair, wishing I could prop my legs up, but settled for lacing my hands behind my head. "Humor me."

Colt rubbed his chin, thinking for a moment before speaking. "If shifters could be summed up in a single word, it would be pride. We're proud of being part of the animal kingdom in ways that normal humans have broken away from. But that pride has also been our downfall. It might be what wipes us out."

"Why do you say that?"

"Because we're too proud to ask for help," he said with a small smile. "To reach out to others outside of our species and especially to humans. Our ancestors said we didn't need shamans anymore, so they stopped passing on their gifts. As the number of shaman dwindled, shifters became even more closed off to humans and isolated themselves in their own communities. Without shaman, the general human population became less educated about shifters. Which is why we're hunted down to the extent that we are today."

He punctuated his monologue with a shrug. "At least that's my theory, anyway."

"So Mel is leading a new movement, in a sense." I rubbed my jaw. "She's saving shifters and also taking them as mates. That would probably blow the socks off the general human population if they knew."

"Shifters *and* normal humans as mates." Colt motioned toward me. "But yes, she's already normalizing shifter-kind. We're animals, but we're also people. Ultimately, we're not that different."

"Be honest now," I told him. "How would you feel if Miriam started seeing another human?"

He made a displeased face that made me laugh out loud. "No offense, Connor. But most humans aren't like you. All I can think of is some fuckin' redneck hillbilly sweating and moaning on top of her."

"What about another shaman?"

He shrugged, his face resuming a look of neutrality. "It's not very likely. Shaman are so few and far between now. Plus, most of them are female." He grinned. "That might be fun, but I don't think she'd like us taking attention away from her. It would depend on the situation, of course."

"Definitely. Hey," I directed my wheelchair to the fridge and opened, pleased to see that no one had touched my six-pack. I grabbed one beer and tossed it to Colt. "We have some kids to watch, don't we?"

"We do," he chuckled, leading the way out to the back porch and holding the door open for me. "Listen, Connor," he began, pausing to open his can and sip the foam that bubbled over the top.

"Yeah?" I watched him curiously.

He took a seat on the lawn chair next to me, resting the beer on his knee as he watched the kids run across the lawn. Even the littlest one, Riley, shrieked with laughter as she chased a grinning Roo. He kept his pace slow and let her tag him. He then gave her plenty of distance as she tore off on her chubby, wobbly legs before giving chase.

For the hundredth time that day, I wished Mel was here. She would have died from happiness seeing this.

"I respect the hell out of you," Colt said finally. "And Mel. It doesn't matter to me one bit that y'all are human. I'm glad it was you two that saved Hunter. So thank you for that."

"Sure thing, Colt." I held out my fist for him to bump. "I respect you too. Gabe, though? I dunno about that guy."

"He'll come around," Colt laughed, flicking his long, dark hair back with one hand. "Once he extracts his head from his ass."

"Let's hope that happens before I knock his damn head from his shoulders."

"I don't blame you one bit," he chuckled.

We sipped and made commentary on the kids' tag game like a couple of sports announcers until the sun dipped low behind the trees. Cicadas sang their mating call and mosquitos came out in full force, but we couldn't bring ourselves to call the children inside yet.

Exhausted from their game, they sprawled out on the grass and watched the stars come out. Roo and Rinna pointed out constellations and star names they knew to Mel's siblings, telling the myths and stories behind the characters in the sky. Colt and I were also content to sit and listen.

"Damn, they're smart," I muttered, draining the last of my beer.

"They are," Colt agreed proudly. "I didn't even know Hunter taught them all this stuff. He always did love night runs and stargazing though."

I tried not to feel uncomfortable that he had used the past tense, and crushed my beer can in my hand as I turned to go inside.

"Lord almighty, I hope they're all okay down there," I muttered.

MELODY

Lhozen wasn't in his office when my guards dragged me back to that fancy, wood-paneled room. Instead, I found a note on the couch where I first woke up that said,

MELODY,

I understand seeing your mates in that state was disturbing for you. Feel free to draw yourself a bath to relax. Then my guards will escort you to dinner, where we will talk more. -Lhozen

WHAT THE JESUS JUMPING FUCK?

I tore my eyes away from the note, then noticed on the end table next to the couch was a folded bathrobe and a varied selection of bath bombs. Against my better judgement, I reached out to touch the dense and insanely soft terry-cloth robe. Yup, definitely never worn before and most likely expensive.

What the hell is his end game here? He can't seriously be trying to bribe me?

I must have stood there for a handful of minutes trying to figure this all out, re-reading the note and looking at the bath stuff like I would find a clue. Nothing came to me, though.

What if I just refuse?

The guards escorting me to dinner sounded like his posh, British way of telling me I had no choice in the matter. Even so, what the hell was up with the bath stuff?

Like they were covered in some infectious disease, I lifted the robe and bath bombs off the table. No matter how badly I wanted to burn this place to the ground, it would be easier for me and everyone else involved if I played along. At least for now.

I tried a few different doors in the office. Most of them didn't budge, but the bathroom opened easily. It was just as luxurious as the office—an open floor plan with a claw-foot tub, spotless white tiles and plush bath mats under foot.

I scanned the room for anything that might resemble a camera lens. Lhozen didn't seem like *that* kind of pervert, but I wouldn't rule it out.

When nothing stood out to me, I turned the handles on the tub and removed my clothes. Deciding not to use the bath bombs in case they were laced with a poison or some type of drug, I set them aside and turned to hang the bathrobe on the door. To my surprise, the door already had an outfit hanging on the hook, and the sight of it made me stop in my tracks.

It was a red dress. Not just any dress, but an evening gown. It was strapless, the bodice form-fitting like a corset with a skirt that flares out at the hips. My heart sank. I had no doubt Lhozen wanted me to wear it to dinner. The strappy black heels on the floor confirmed it like the final nail in my coffin.

I sank into the scalding water of the tub when it filled, keeping my back turned to the door so I wouldn't have to look at that dress. I scrubbed at my skin, trying to erase the disgusting feeling that came over me. It felt just like when I performed with Syko for the first time. Like I served no purpose but to be arm candy. I had been nothing but a dolled-up prop for the most vile human being on earth.

I stayed in the tub until the water got cold. If I was late or early, I had no idea. Lhozen's note never specified a time, and I wondered if he'd want to punish me for making him wait.

Better me than my guys, I thought as I slowly toweled off. As if he didn't have the ability to hurt all of us at the same time. The despair began as a tiny doubt that snowballed, growing more and more as I took the dress off the hanger and stepped into it. I couldn't bring myself to look in the mirror, not even when I brushed my hair or applied lotion from an unopened bottle on the vanity. Lhozen's fancy bathroom didn't seem to supply makeup, so I didn't bother with any.

The dress and shoes fit perfectly, which only made me feel shittier. How could he have known my size? Maybe he was a god, and we were all just fooling ourselves.

Despite the perfect fit, I couldn't twist my arms enough to finish zipping up the damn thing. Sighing heavily, I opened the bathroom door only halfway zipped. When I returned to the office, my guards were waiting.

"Can you zip me?" I asked, turning around and lifting my hair off my neck.

Nothing happened for a long moment. I almost thought they would keep standing there like a statue, but soon felt leather-gloved fingertips skim the small of my back in search of the zipper. They snapped it up so hard I thought the zipper might break. And then thankfully the feeling of leather was gone.

"Thanks," I muttered, turning around.

The guard gave a curt nod and, for the first time, I looked at his face. Like, really looked at him as a person. He wasn't ugly. Probably in his early forties, clean-shaven, with hard, stern eyes. His cheeks were tinged with pink, probably at having to touch me.

The thought of trying to seduce him crossed my mind and made me recoil instantly. Even if it was a successful means to an end, I couldn't look my men in the face after betraying them like that. My mom and older sister used sex to get what they wanted. I would never be that person.

"Are we done here?" snapped the other guard by the door.

"Yeah," I drawled in the same indignant tone. "We're done."

The guard who zipped me took hold of my arm. My fresh bruises stood out in reddish purple welts on my pale skin, and I noticed he avoided closing his hand over them. He also didn't squeeze as hard as the other guy, who made me hiss in pain from his yanking my arm. Yup, that was the shoulder that had almost been dislocated. Left Guard was a grade-A asshole.

As they led me out of the office and into the now-familiar hallway, my eyes flickered to Zipper Guard on my right. Seducing him was out of the question, but maybe befriending him wouldn't be a bad idea. Surely not everyone here agreed with whatever Lhozen's sadistic plan was, right?

"What's your name?" I tried.

"Don't get chatty, bitch," barked Asshole Guard. "You stay quiet unless you're spoken to, understand?"

"I wasn't talking to you," I retorted cattily.

He replied with a yank on my arm that had me yelping and fresh tears springing to my eyes. He pulled so hard, my other arm came out of Zipper Guard's grip, and Asshole shook me like a rag doll.

"Bitch, say one more goddamn word and I swear to God, I'll—"

"Renson, stop." Zipper braced his arm between us. "If she talks, just ignore her. We need to take her to him in one piece."

Asshole released me with a growl, grinding his teeth with a wild look in his beady eyes. Something was wrong with that guy. He wanted to hurt something just for the sake of hurting it; he obviously liked inflicting pain.

"He's right," Zipper muttered once we resumed our walk. "You're better off not asking any questions."

THE WALK ENDED through one of the many unmarked doors in the hallway. I had no idea how any of Lhozen's minions kept from getting lost in this maze, but what laid out on the other side was unlike anything I'd ever seen.

It reminded me of the dining room from Beauty and the Beast. A long dinner table with elegant chairs and a chandelier overhead. Lhozen was already seated, while wait staff whisked in and out of the room.

"Your chair, miss?" A man in a tuxedo swept his hand toward a chair directly next to Lhozen and looked at me expectantly. I returned his look with one of, *what the fuck is going on?*

This place almost felt like a twilight zone with rooms like this, and his office hiding behind metal doors. Was any of this actually here, or were these things more of Lhozen's illusions? Was this whole compound based on something that wasn't real? My head pounded with trying to make sense of what was real or fake.

My guys. Their lives and their safety. They're real and that's what matters.

"Melody, please sit," Lhozen motioned toward me. It sounded like an invitation, but I heard the undertone of a command. "You must be starving."

I had no appetite, actually. I was pretty certain my stomach was empty, and I still wanted to vomit all over this dress that probably cost an arm and a leg.

Nonetheless, I marched over and took a seat while the man in a tuxedo politely pushed my chair in. Immediately, a stemmed glass was placed in front of me and wine began pouring into it.

"I don't drink," I said, holding my hand out. "I'm too young, anyway."

"Ah. A pity." Lhozen signaled to the waiter, and the glass was whisked away. "But you are just in time for the main course."

A steaming plate was placed in front of me and despite my lack of appetite, my mouth watered. My plate held the juiciest steak I'd ever seen, cooked to a perfect medium, flanked by buttered potatoes and roasted vegetables. It looked too good to eat.

That's because it's not real, I reminded myself. It can't be real. Nothing he offers you is real.

I could feel Lhozen's eyes on me as I stared at my plate. The whole situation felt very Hannibal Lecter to me. What was *really* on my plate? Just to be safe, I picked up a fork and poked at the vegetables.

"You're suspicious," Lhozen observed. "Very cautious. That's one of the reasons why I chose you to receive the gift of the shaman. The best casters of Semblance also know how to look for illusions."

I brought a carrot to my mouth and chewed slowly. Holy shit, it was really good. Coated in some kind of glaze and cooked to perfection as it melted in my mouth. Maybe it *was* real?

"But you're still young and your power is unrestrained," he went on. "You need more training and I need my work to continue while I am not long for this world."

That took me by surprise. I swallowed the carrot and tried to regard him calmly, as difficult as it was. My other hand clenched in my lap, because it was all I could do not to reach across the table and choke him.

"What do you mean by that?" I asked.

"It means I don't have long to live, dear." He gave me a sad smile. "Although I've lived many lives, as you know. I'm quite certain I've seen the world through the eyes of every creature imaginable. From a praying mantis to a blue whale. It's simply marvelous this magic we have." He paused and gave me a strange look. "But I've seen nothing more lovely than looking through the eyes of a certain wolf, tiger, and dragon."

My hand froze in shock as I was moving a piece of potato to my mouth. Only through sheer force of will did I continue its trajectory past my lips. I chewed as slowly as I could with my pulse hammering in my veins.

So he *was* that kind of pervert. Only instead of looking through hidden cameras, he looked through the eyes of shifters. And not just any shifters. Mine. Private moments with my men and he was there like a sick little peeping tom. I don't know how I didn't throw up right then.

This information was important. My brain buzzed for a moment, trying to make a connection, then it hit me.

Arjun knew.

Of course, that brilliant, beautiful tiger fucking knew.

He couldn't tell me directly, not with the risk of Lhozen seeing through him and hearing his words. That was why he wouldn't do anything beyond kissing me. He didn't want to give this pervert the sick satisfaction of seeing us together. It had to be why he said that ring-mistress stuff. I still didn't know what that meant, but I finally knew something I didn't before. Lhozen's ego was just too big to keep it to himself.

I forced a smile at him, hoping he didn't see the epiphany that just went off in my head.

"You saw through my men, intentionally?" I asked, forcing my voice not to shake.

"I did. And what a sight it was."

"How?" I propped my elbow on the table and rested my chin in my hand, hoping I made a convincing show of looking interested. "I've never been able to control the shifters I see through. Sometimes I'm watching a hunt. Other times I'm witnessing a private moment between two lovers that should only be between them."

I probably shouldn't have been snarky, but I couldn't help it.

"Under my training, you'll learn all that and more," he promised, ignoring my snark. "What do you say, Melody?"

"You ask that like I have a choice in the matter," I remarked.

"Because I'm a gentleman," he said with a smile. "But truthfully, no. You don't."

18

MELODY

"So what is the alternative?"

Lhozen gave me an eerily calm, patronizing smile. "My dear, if you truly had any idea, you would not dare to ask that question."

I set my fork down and brought my hands to my lap, trying to look as docile and cooperative as possible.

"Can I just ask... that you please not hurt them?" My lip wobbled. "Don't drug them. Don't force them to shift. If you could even consider letting them go—"

"Now why would I do that?" he mused arrogantly. "When they've so eagerly returned to me?"

The silence stretched between us. His glassy blue eyes never left mine, daring me to challenge him. With every interaction we had, I was beginning to see there was no reasoning with him.

"Don't hurt them then," I relented in a small voice. "Please."

"Since you asked so nicely, I'll consider it." He rose from the table, his dismissive tone made it perfectly clear he would do no such thing. "Now, come with me to the parlor, dear."

He held his arm out to me, bent at a ninety-degree angle. I swallowed my discomfort as I pushed my chair back and stood, my food mostly untouched while his plate was empty. The wait staff immediately swarmed in like an ant colony to clear the table. After placing my hand on his awaiting arm, Lhozen wasted no time in leading me away through another door.

This one led to another room of old-world elegance, just like the dining room. A classical quartet played soft background music in the corner. An elaborate bar made of glossy dark wood stood against one wall, surrounded by glittering crystal bottles of every size and shape imaginable. This room was, for the most part, empty and open. There were a few plush couches and armchairs scattered around, but the massive size of the room made it feel sparsely decorated.

"Dance with me." Lhozen turned me around and placed a hand on my waist. He made it clear that it wasn't a request.

I followed his lead to the middle of the room, then again as he took my hand and began moving to the classical music.

His eyes were half-closed, top lids lightly fluttering as we moved around the room. I could only guess he was focusing hard on some illusion, but what? And for what purpose?

My eyes slid around the room as we twirled. Aside from us, the band, and my guards, no one else was in the room. No one was watching. Why cast such elaborate illusions if there was no one to impress?

"You're a natural dancer," he murmured, extending his arm out to twirl me away. I played along, even flashing him a smile as I twirled back into his arms. I always was good at fake smiles when I was uncomfortable.

The music picked up speed and Lhozen went right along with it. I did my best to keep up, my mind still reeling as I tried to make sense of this whole act. He at first maintained a polite distance between us. Still, the longer we danced, I realized he drew me in closer and closer.

My belly brushed against his, and that hand on my waist pressed into me like a wall. I started to panic, my eyes darting about the room, hoping to catch the eyes of the others here. *Zipper Guard, my friend! Help me!*

Our gazes did meet as Lhozen continued twirling me around the room, but there was something weird about both of my guards.

Their eyes followed me watchfully, but instead of expressing anything, they stared with empty, hypnotic gazes.

I looked back at Lhozen, his face inches from mine now. His eyes were opened wider than before, but held the same blank stare as my guards. He wore a relaxed half-smile, as if sitting back on a sunny day and watching clouds go by.

Now thoroughly freaked out, it took me a full minute of twirling for it all to fall into place in my brain.

I was a ringmistress.

And this was just another performance.

My mind flew back to my burlesque dance when Raz and I rescued Arjun. Everyone watching me perform had been caught in a trance. They had been oblivious to anything else until Arjun jumped off the stage and mauled half the people watching.

Now the exact same thing was happening. I took my hand off Lhozen's shoulder and snapped my fingers in front of his face.

Nothing. His body kept moving us through the dance, but his eyes saw nothing but me.

Arjun, I will do so much more than kiss you when we get out of here.

Lhozen released me to do another twirl and this time I put extra flair in it, kicking one leg up to show off my calf under the puffy red skirt. At the same time, I looked around the room for a more thorough inspection.

Only the band in the corner didn't seem affected by my dance. Their eyes remained focused on their instruments as they played tirelessly. They had to be an illusion. There was no other explanation, even if they seemed so lifelike. Even if I was wrong, I had to risk it at this point.

Spinning around, the room with Lhozen, my eyes settled on the tranquilizer guns in my guards' holsters. That was it. My only shot.

I didn't dare interrupt the flow of the dance for fear of taking them out of their stupor, so I waited. We did three more rotations around the room before circling back to where we were closest to the guarded doors. My heart nearly vibrated from pounding so fast and my feet were starting to protest. I wondered if I let this go on, if Lhozen would keep dancing until he dropped dead.

But I couldn't wait that long, nor risk dropping dead myself. So when he extended his arm to let me twirl away once again, I took my chance.

I pulled my fingers out of his grip and continued

twirling on my own, flashing him a flirtatious smile as I spun closer and closer to Asshole Guard. Looking back over my shoulder, he watched me with a dazed smile, and my heart leaped with victory. The trance was holding.

My spinning stopped directly in front of my guard and I extended my palm to him with a smile, as if asking him for the next dance. He returned the smile, removing his hand from his belt to accept the invitation. And then I shattered the illusion like a rock through a window.

My hand dove for his holster, wrapping my hand around the grip of the gun, and pulled. It came out easily, thank Jesus, but felt as heavy as a brick in my small, shaking hands.

Asshole Guard only had a moment to blink dumbly at me before I pointed at his chest and squeezed the trigger. A dart shot out, hitting him right in the pectoral muscle with nothing more than the sound of a small puff of air.

I didn't wait for his reaction, but stepped out of his reach and spun around to point the gun at Lhozen. My second shot hit him in the stomach, which he looked at in confusion. A thump behind me confirmed that the guard went down, and I glanced over my shoulder at Zipper Guard.

He still seemed dazed, blinking rapidly as his hands hovered over his own gun as if to pull it out.

"Sorry," I muttered, before aiming and pulling my trigger for a third time. The dart hit him in the shoulder.

"Shit," he groaned before slumping against the wall, fighting to keep his legs under him, but the tranquilizer was already circulating through his system.

When I turned back to Lhozen, he was on his knees and struggling to stay conscious. I didn't know how many darts were left in the gun, but would they kill him if I emptied the rest into him? Tempting as it was, I still had to free my guys. Plus, he was Arjun's to deal with.

"You...won't..." he slurred, fighting the sedative to lift his head up and shoot me a look of pure rage.

He finally collapsed, and the whole room shifted, like looking at a holographic image from another angle. The quartet band had disappeared, replaced by a vintage record player. A slow spinning vinyl album that played the same classical music as the illusioned band had been.

The bar, furniture, and all the elegant touches of the room disappeared, exposing the cold, empty room underneath. It looked like some kind of hospital storage room, stark white and sterile, with a few stainless steel cabinets, but not much else.

Unfortunately, my ridiculous dress and shoes were very real.

After spending precious seconds just staring at my new surroundings, I grabbed Zipper Guard's gun from his holster. In a moment of quick thinking, I grabbed his access badge too and shoved it down the front of my dress.

Now unguarded with two heavy-as-fuck tranq guns and standing out like a sore thumb in my puffy red dress, I pushed the door ajar with my shoulder. Poking my head out to look both ways down the hallway, I walked out when the coast was clear.

My heels clicked softly, echoing off the metal doors and walls as I headed back to the caged area. I held both guns at my sides, index fingers on each trigger and ready to pull.

Don't worry, guys, I thought. Your shaman's coming.

19

MELODY

I walked the hall alone in silence until I reached the long window that looked down over the warehouse full of cages below. Pressing myself to the wall, I had to bunch up my skirt so none of the humans would see it as I peeked through.

Only four humans in lab coats were down there, sitting around the metal table in the center. Two were typing on laptops, one flipped through charts, the other just leaned against the table, chatting. He was the least distracted and, therefore, the biggest threat.

I spotted Raz and Hunter in their cage, pushed back into a dark corner. Raz, still covered in black scales, was barely visible in the shadows. Hunter's form stood out as stark white, with a dark, shadowy form wrapped around him.

Raz, Hunter, I thought. *Don't react, but I escaped. I have two tranq guns and an access card. I can see you guys through the top window.*

My eyes fluttered halfway closed as I sent my presence

to them. My dragon and my wolf received my presence in their heads with a flood of relief and warm, loving emotions.

Steluţa, I've never been so happy to hear you and feel you, Raz returned.

Are you guys okay? How's Hunter?

We're both okay. They haven't given us anything since the forced-shifting drugs when you were last here. We still can't shift either way, though. This shit lasts around twenty-four hours.

Are those four humans the only ones here? What's the best way for me to get you guys out?

Yes, but you need to get them away from the desk. There's an alarm button underneath. If they push that, everyone in this compound will come running. I saw them test it last time I was here.

Okay. Can you guys distract them? Maybe get at least one of them to approach your cage?

I'll do what I can, but they might stick us with more drugs.

I have an idea. Just get one of them to approach you.

Okay, my love.

I pulled away from the window, flattening myself against the wall to take deep breaths. As I heard the loud clang of bars down below, I closed my eyes and focused on the illusion.

My red dress became dark green fatigues from head to toe, the strappy black heels shifting into combat boots. And on my belt, an empty holster where I could pretend to fit one of my guns. I pulled the brim of the matching green hat low over my eyes and walked confidently in front of the window.

All four humans now had their attention focused on Raz, banging on his bars and snarling. His jaws gnashed, showing off his pointed dragon teeth as he let out incomprehensible grunts and growls. Knowing him, he was throwing out curses and insults, but because of his partial shift, they couldn't understand him.

"Jesus, will you make it shut the fuck up?" one of the humans said as I reached the top of the stairs and began my descent.

"Happily," another one muttered, reaching for the tranq gun at her hip as she approached the cage. "How many should I empty into him?"

"Give him at least four," laughed another, the one who had been standing and talking.

"No way, he's a dragon. If he dies, our asses are on the line."

They bickered and bantered as I descended the staircase with the softest steps I could manage, desperate to not make my heels click and ruin the illusion. None of them paid any mind as I approached the table, running my fingers just underneath the lip until I found the button. The fucking chatty guy was standing right next to it.

"What's up?" he said, turning to me with a curious look. "Aren't you supposed to be guarding the chick?"

I lifted my gaze to his, ensuring that he saw my face under the brim of the hat, but didn't wait to see his expression transform. I pressed the barrel of the gun against his chest and squeezed the trigger. The moment the dart released, I shoved him backward and took his place to stand right in front of the alarm button.

"Guysssss...," was all he could get out before going down.

The remaining three turned back to me. One guy took

off running, and I shot at him twice, the darts going wild. Shooting again, the third one sank into his back.

"Aaaahh, no! Let us go!"

The other two, both women, had gotten close enough to Raz's cage for him to grab them through the bars. They struggled and fought, but my dragon held an arm around one's waist and the other's neck. I lifted my gun and aimed, but the trigger clicked uselessly when I pulled.

"Fuck." I dropped it on the table and raised the other one, catching each of them in the chest with a clean, single shot.

You're good with that thing, steluța, Raz praised.

"Thanks, dragon." I shoved the slumped bodies of the humans out of my way as I unlocked his cage with my stolen access badge.

We barely had time to open the barrier between us and fall into each other's arms when my head was assaulted with voices and visions.

IS THAT THE SHAMAN? IS SHE GOING TO SAVE US?

SHAMAN! LET US OUT!

SHAMAN, MY CHILDREN! PLEASE SAVE MY BABIES!

"Agh, God!" I collapsed into a crumpled heap, my guard illusion now gone as I clutched my head. Every voice was like a hammer cracking through my skull.

Steluța!

"No, don't!" I cried, shaking my head. "Don't talk to me in my head! Fuck, it hurts so fucking bad..."

I wanted to throw up. To bang my head against the bars. To shoot myself with the tranq gun just to make it all stop. Every time this had happened before was nothing compared to this. Every single cry and plea, every desperate voice felt like a sledgehammer was splitting my brain apart.

Somehow, I saw through the unfathomable pain to put the key card into Raz's scaled, clawed hand.

"Get Arjun," I whimpered. "Get him out."

Then I pressed the tranq gun to my chest and fired.

20

ARJUN

When the flames on the floor of my cell disappeared, I didn't stop holding my breath. Lhozen liked to play games. He liked to *test my strength,* as he called it.

Even after Mel proved to me the flames were an illusion, I couldn't make myself face them. My closet-sized prison cell was four blank walls and those flames. There was nothing else to focus on but them and my fear.

I tried to remember jumping through Raz's fire onstage with him—real flames. Granted, he cooled their temperature and taught me to jump safely, but every practice run with him was a leap of faith. A headfirst jump directly into my fear.

The difference was, I trusted Raz. I could face my fear, because I knew my friend would be on the other side.

I used to trust Lhozen too, but not anymore.

He used these flames as a weapon against me, a tool to break me, to make me an obedient little cat. I wanted to laugh. To tell him to his face that he'd never break me down again, because I found someone to lift me up.

A girl born in a trailer park in Alabama, who had a stick up her arse at my sense of humor and made tea in the fucking microwave.

She wasn't the mate I had expected, but the gorgeous shaman from the shittiest upbringing was more than I could have ever dreamed of. I loved Melody and would never get the chance to show her.

Because as the hours rolled on and those imaginary flames rose higher, my stepfather succeeded in breaking me down.

I curled into a pathetic little ball in the corner of my cell as they stretched across the floor. The heat licking at my skin was too much. I had already screamed my throat raw and couldn't wrap my arms any tighter around myself. My sanity was unraveling.

When the flames disappeared, I knew it was only a matter of time before they'd return. Lhozen would wait until I was lulled into a false sense of security before bringing them back—probably directly on my skin next time.

The minutes ticked by and my paranoia grew. I could hear what sounded like yelling on the other side of my metal door, but chalked them up to hallucinations. Frightened out of my mind of what might come next, it made sense for my brain to create distractions.

When I heard the telltale beep of an access card and my door began sliding open, I knew I was losing it.

"Arrrj." The black, demon-like hallucination growled as he approached.

"Well done, Lhozen." I brought my hands together in a

half-hearted clap. "You've won. If Hell exists, I hope demons just like this one fuck you in the arse for all eternity."

"Arrrj!" The creature roared more insistently as he stopped right in front of my face. Damn, he certainly looked real. His clawed, scaly, black hands grabbed my shoulders and gave them a solid shake. Then he slapped me.

It wasn't hard, but was familiar enough to make me look up at his face. He had done it almost in an affectionate way, like a friend would.

Those eyes. Why did this reptilian creature look so familiar?

"Arrrj!" He shook me again. "Sss-raz. Merrrl-dee heerrr."

"Raz?" I blinked. "Raz, that's you?"

He slapped me again and roared victoriously as he pulled me to my feet.

"Wait." I braced against his arms, holding myself up. "Why aren't you using Mel's Speak?"

He stretched his jaws, flashing teeth that rivaled the ferocity and deadliness of my tiger.

"Seee hurrrr." He formed one hand into a gun and pointed it directly at his own chest.

"She's hurt?"

He nodded emphatically. "Shuffft-terz." He clapped his clawed hands to the sides of his head and made a display of being in great pain.

"Of course, the shifters," I breathed, following him dumbfounded out of the cell. "She would feel them right here stronger than at any point before."

He led me to where she laid motionless and propped

up in the furry white arms of Hunter, who rocked her gently.

My heart stopped as I ran over to them. "Gods, no! Is she…?"

"Sllleerp." Hunter pointed to the tranquilizer gun, and I sagged with relief.

"Fucking hell. This place is hard enough to escape without her knocked out and you two sounding like cave trolls."

"Narrllawffuh, Arrrj."

"I know it's not your fault, mate," I answered Raz as I inspected the rest of the humans lying on the ground. All out cold. "Would just be a lot easier if I didn't have to infer what the bloody hell you're saying."

I checked over a guy who looked about my height and proceeded to strip his pants off his legs. *Sorry mate, I need these more than you.* "How the hell did you knock all of them out?"

"Merrll drr," Raz inclined his horned head toward Mel. I only then noticed she was in a bright red ballgown. The puffy skirt spread about her and Hunter like a cloud.

"Right." I shook my head, still in disbelief that I hadn't been burned alive. "They must have adrenaline here to counteract the sedatives. No idea if they have anything for you blokes, sorry."

"Serrkuh."

He was either saying *it's okay* or *suck my dick*, neither of which warranted a response as I scanned the shelves lined with small glass bottles. Most of their labels had long pharmaceutical names, and I didn't have a clue how they worked.

All the while, I felt the intensity of hundreds of eyes staring at me. I couldn't hear them, but I knew the shifters in this room were mentally screaming at Mel, pleading for their lives. The moment I saw the adrenaline, I grabbed the whole case of bottles. They would fit into the same cartridge as the tranquilizers for the guns.

"Listen up," I said, turning to address the audience of caged shifters in the room. "There's no time for pleasantries. The lot of you need to shut the fuck up."

I got some head tilts and pawing at their bars, but whatever response they had, I couldn't hear.

"The girl is a shaman and we will all help you escape," I went on. "But you can't bombard her head with pleas and cries and begging. You must trust us. You must allow her to focus on her abilities. But I promise you, we will leave no one behind."

With that, I popped the adrenaline cartridge into the empty gun on the table and returned to where Mel was slumped against Hunter in the cage.

I pressed the gun to her chest and hesitated. "I'm sorry if this hurts, dove." And squeezed the trigger.

Her eyes shot open after a few seconds and her hands immediately went up to the sides of her head. "No, no, I can't be awake."

"Easy, dove." I dropped the gun and pulled her forward, immediately shifting to allow my purr to calm and soothe her. "You're alright. I told them to shut the fuck up. If they're still bothering you, Raz and Hunter will give them something to be scared of."

"Arjun?" she looked up at me, blinking as if unbelieving I was there.

"Yes, it's me, my love."

"You're free!" Her arms wrapped around my neck and her lips found mine.

Kissing her erased the last of my fear that still lingered from my metal box. I crushed her to my chest, feeling her heart against my own, and just relished in the joy of tasting her. My mate. My love.

But I couldn't let go and enjoy her as fully as I would have liked, knowing he could be seeing through me, Hunter, Raz, or any shifter in this place.

"Mel," I rasped, pulling away with regret. "Where's Lhozen, dove? What happened?"

"I knocked him out," she told me, a slight pant in her voice. "He's in a room upstairs, unconscious. I shot him and my guards with tranqs."

"Good girl," I praised, smoothing her hair away from her face. Unable to help myself, I kissed her again before resting my forehead on hers. "I knew you could. As cynical a bastard as I am, I knew you'd find a way."

"Arjun." Her expression turned grave as she licked her lips. "Something's... wrong with him. I don't know what, but he's completely delusional. He dressed me up like this, made a show of a fancy dinner and dancing for no reason. It's almost like he lives entirely in illusions and has forgotten about reality."

"I see." I measured her words carefully. "But you left him alive for me?"

"I did." A wicked grin came across her beautiful face. "He's all yours."

"Good. Up you go. Our work isn't done here."

Mel, Hunter, and I exited the cage to find Raz loading more tranquilizers into guns and setting them on the table.

Found their stash, he chuckled amusedly, then gave me a pointed look. *Can you hear me now?*

"I can, Raz." I answered, squeezing Mel's nape. "I had a hell of a time trying to communicate with these wankers while you were out, dove."

"Sorry I missed that," she muttered, dark eyes flashing as she watched me load another adrenaline cartridge into the gun I had just used on her. "You going to wake him up?"

"Yeah." I double checked the weapon before observing all the guns and cartridges laid out on the table. "Think you three can hold the fort here while I'm dealing with him?"

We have enough tranquilizers to bring down a herd of buffalo, so I think we can manage any more humans wandering in here, Raz observed.

"So we'll start unlocking cages and giving First Aid to those who need it," Mel said before glancing back at me. "And finding a way for everyone to get out of here, while you're busy."

"It's a plan." I slid a hand across her lower back and pulled her in for another kiss, sending my tongue past her lips this time, now that I knew Lhozen was unconscious and couldn't see.

"Be careful," she told me solemnly, giving me a hard look. "And don't hesitate to call me if you need backup." She tapped her temple, and I kissed her there, too.

"I will," I promised her. "But I'll tell you right now, I'll be taking my time with him. There are things he needs to answer for."

She nodded in understanding and let me go to start removing access badges from the unconscious humans.

Shove a sword down his throat for me, Raz called after me as I jogged up the stairs.

"Oh, I'll make him wish for that," I promised.

21

ARJUN

I pulled open five of those bloody metal doors before I found him. He and the two guards were lying where Mel left them, sprawled out on the floor. Standing over his body, I took a moment to look at my stepfather before shooting him full of adrenaline.

He definitely looked older than when I last saw him. I remembered my first few months in captivity, yearning for the days he'd sit with me and Mum over tea. He told stories of the shaman from years before and their shifter companions. One thing I always remembered vividly was how strongly he felt about humans and shifters coexisting peacefully.

He adored and loved Mum so much. My own father left our family to pursue another tigress who he felt was his true mate. Lhozen never treated me like a member of a different species. He affectionately called me son and filled every role that a father should.

At least he did until Mum died.

I yanked the empty tranquilizer cartridge out of his

belly and pressed the gun against the same spot. The trigger pull made his whole body jerk from the impact. Then I sat back on my heels and waited.

His eyes shot open, blinking rapidly before he rubbed them with a heavy groan.

"Hello, Lhozen," I greeted.

"Arjun," he said with what almost sounded like pleasant surprise as he pushed himself up.

With a quick shove to his shoulder, I laid him flat on his back again with a grunt.

"I like you better like this, I think." My teeth ground together as I spoke and my index finger danced along the trigger of the gun. How tempting it was just to make his heart explode with adrenaline and end this bullshit now.

"This isn't exactly proper, is it?" he complained, but didn't try to sit up again. "Why don't we chat over tea like adults?"

"Why don't you stay exactly where you are?" I suggested, waving the gun in front of his face. "And explain to me what's proper about rounding up shifters, keeping them in cages, and pumping them full of drugs?"

"Really now, Arjun?" he sighed as if incredulous.

"Yes, really," I demanded, willing my voice not to crack. "How could you love Mum and treat others like this? How could you call me a son and do this to *me?*"

"Because you're being short-sighted and not seeing the whole picture!" he spat. "You don't see the vision that I do, the world in which your kind become the saviors of humanity."

Mel was right. He really was delusional. "What the bloody hell are you talking about?"

"Come on, Arjun. You're not daft. Look at the

numbers, the data. The number one killer of humans is heart disease. Then diabetes, then cancer. How many shifters have died from those diseases?"

"Probably none because humans kill us first."

"Exactly, none! When was the last time you had a cold? The whole time you were in captivity, did you ever fall ill?"

My stomach seemed to turn in on itself, bile building up in my throat. "That's why you did it? As an experiment?"

"The human race is killing itself, Arjun. Shifters are thriving and hiding in plain sight. We can coexist, but us humans must save ourselves first."

"By enslaving us?!" I demanded. "What about Razvan the dragon, remember him? Hunter the Wolf Man? What's the greater good for exhibiting them like freaks?"

"Not all experiments are successful. The... uncooperative ones cannot be returned home, for risk of retribution against me from their communities."

I shook my head, unable to believe this was a real conversation happening between us. "You've truly lost your mind. Mum would be horrified at what you've done. I can't make heads or tails of whatever you're trying to do."

"Your mum," he whispered, his eyes becoming watery. "She would be proud of me."

"No, she fucking wouldn't."

"I miss her so much," he went on as if he didn't hear me. "When I gather enough data on shifter genetics, I may be able to bring her back."

My eyes nearly fell out of my head. "You what?"

"I still have a lock of her hair," his hand clamored up to the breast pocket of his jacket. "Cloning is more difficult with a mixture of animal and human DNA. I've already tried a few times. But when she returns to us, Arjun," he swept a hand, and the room transformed into an elegant parlor, the mirror image of the one we used to have back at home, "everything needs to be as it was before she was taken from us."

I could only gawk at my stepfather in disbelief. The only explanation I could fathom was that he snapped after she died. Like Mel said, his whole life became one big illusion. Coupled with his drinking, it must have driven him to avoid his grief, his new reality without her.

And hundreds, if not thousands, of shifters had suffered for it.

"You cannot get in my way, Arjun," he said, pushing himself up to sitting once again. "I've always loved you like my own son, but you and that girl cannot stop what must be done."

Something bright flickered at the corner of my eye and I yelped, dropping the gun and jumping away as my whole left arm became engulfed in flames.

I slapped my arm against the floor and rolled around desperately in my panic. *No, no, no! Put it out, I'm going to die!*

Even in my crazy desperation, my mind registered seeing Lhozen climbing to his feet, and it jogged a recent memory. Large dark eyes, raven black hair, and gentle hands on my skin. A voice telling me it wasn't real.

Only my fear made it real.

I forced myself to be still, holding my arm out in front of me. The flames danced and flickered, casting light and heat, but my arm was not burning.

Mel, you amazing, beautiful woman, you've saved me. You've saved us all.

My other hand unsnapped my pants, and I stepped out

of them. I didn't even have to think about shifting. My tiger rose to the surface as easily as breathing. His was the blood we needed to spill since the beginning. Vengeance for our kind and our family.

"Lhozen," I growled, striding toward him while I could still walk upright. My teeth already pointed past my lips and stripes erupted on my skin.

He turned, nearly falling on his ass again when he saw that preying on my fear didn't work. My arm, now fire-free, lifted and pointed a long, curled claw at him.

"We arrrre stopping you," I said around my long teeth and tongue. "This ends with *yourrrr* blood."

I completed my shift and pounced.

My paws on his back sent him crashing down with a pitiful scream. I extended my claws and raked downward, enjoying the stretch while I turned his skin to bloody red ribbons.

He screamed so fucking loud, wailing like a banshee, but I didn't want to bite his throat yet. I wanted to make him feel just an ounce of the suffering he imparted on me for four long years. For everything he had done to Raz. And to Hunter. To Roo and Rinna. And every shifter that hadn't survived his cruelty.

I grabbed his ankle between my jaws and thrashed my head back and forth. Something snapped and his screams took on a new, higher pitch while his leg flopped around uselessly.

Shaking him until I was bored, I licked my lips and purred contentedly as I walked a slow, lazy circle around him. *What shall I break next?*

"Your soul will never be saved for doing this," he whimpered. "You'll be reborn as a parasite. You'll never undo the harm you've done!"

It's already too late for me, I thought. *But it fills me with joy to know you'll never be saved, either.*

I meant that in the spiritual and physical sense. His screams could be heard across the compound, yet no one had come running to his rescue. Granted, any remaining humans were probably lying unconscious in the cage room.

The thought made me pause before taking another bite out of Lhozen's other leg.

I shouldn't be enjoying this alone, I realized. *The others deserve to take their own vengeance, too.*

With that, I grabbed his trouser leg between my teeth, careful not to pierce his flesh, and began dragging him toward the door.

"No, no! Where are you taking me?" he cried pitifully.

I ignored him, leaving a trail of blood as I pulled him along the floor to the hallway. He was not a small man and dragging him was somewhat cumbersome, but I reached the top of the stairs within a few minutes.

Down below, the scene was chaos.

Birds screeched and flew in circles around the room. A bear stood on her hind legs and roared, her cubs greedily nursing from her. Lynxes and foxes yowled as they ran around the room. Mel sat at the center table, tending to some minor wounds on a coyote; Julian, I presumed.

Lhozen let out a cry of pain and the room went silent, all eyes turning to me. Mel smiled, but her eyes held questions.

I placed a paw on Lhozen's shoulder and let out a victorious roar.

I had my words with him, I told Mel. *And spilled the blood I needed to spill. I thought it only fair to share with everyone else.*

None of the shifters responded, so I had no idea if they heard me or not. But Mel turned to address the room and repeat my words.

"Arjun's done with Lhozen," she declared. "He's free for all of you to take a swing, bite or scratch."

"NO! NO! PLEASE!"

His cries were drowned out by the cacophony of the jungle. Even Hunter howled and Raz managed to breathe small puffs of fire. I roared once more. Had I been in human form, I might have beaten my chest. *We won.* I could hardly believe it.

With one shove of my paw, Lhozen went swiftly down the stairs and the mob descended on him. To my surprise, everyone took a turn delivering a non-fatal blow. The larger animals waited patiently for their turn while the smaller ones gnawed, scratched, and swiped at him.

Blood dripped down the stairs, and Lhozen's cries soon turned to meaningless gurgles. I wasn't sure, but I thought one of the birds removed his tongue.

Finally, the she-bear hovered over him after her cubs were done gnawing at his fingers and toes. She stared at him for a long moment, then looked at me and shifted to a blonde woman with a strong, muscular build.

"You deserve the killing blow," she said. "I don't want to take that honor away from you."

I've already taken what I needed. Please, go ahead. Remembering she couldn't hear me, I lowered my head and inclined it to her, prompting her to go ahead with it.

"No, tiger brother." She smiled. "I heard the shaman say he raised you as a father. For you, this won't end here.

You may carry his betrayal as a scar on your heart for the rest of your life. Begin your healing now, by taking away his power."

She stepped away, gathering her cubs to her, and I lowered my head even further in respect. Then I slowly padded down the steps.

Lhozen's face was unrecognizable. His breathing came out soft, wheezing and weak. Whether I finished him or not, he would die soon.

I lifted my gaze to Mel, and she gave me a small, encouraging nod. With a pleased, rumbling purr in my chest, I opened my jaws wide and closed them over his windpipe.

22

MELODY

The compound turned out to be a maze of hallways and tunnels, but with the help of the shifters, we were soon able to locate a discreet exit.

It had been set up to look like a sewage drain that emptied not far from the beach. That only showed how far Lhozen's delusions went. He constructed this whole elaborate place to secretly move shifters in and out, even without using Semblance.

Most of the shifters left immediately, eager to get back to their families, loved ones, and simply enjoy their freedom. A few lingered behind, like Julian and Anya, the she-bear with her cubs.

"Thank you," Julian said shyly for perhaps the hundredth time. "And sorry again, for uh, freaking out while you were talking to me with your mind."

He was utterly adorable. Tall and thin, with a mop of dark hair falling into his eyes. I wanted to adopt him as an older brother.

"Of course. Don't mention it." I said, hugging him around his waist. "If you ever come to Georgia, look me up. We have a big house and will be happy to host you. You too, Anya."

"I'm heading to Canada," she replied with a hint of apology. "Perfect weather up there, plenty of food. Wide open wilderness with fewer humans. No offense."

"None taken," I told her. "Have a safe journey."

"You as well, Melody. Thank you for being one of the good ones. I'll tell my grandchildren about you."

Raz and Hunter were still stuck between their shifts, so I used the last remaining mental focus I had to make them invisible on our walk back to the hotel. Arjun kept mostly silent after killing Lhozen. I wondered if it was bothering him more than he wanted to admit.

My wolf and my dragon collapsed together on the couch the moment we reached the room. With Raz's black scales and Hunter's white fur, they looked like polar opposites, but so perfectly together intertwined. Seeing them together made my heart want to burst. I got so close to losing them, but now they were safe. We were all safe.

I could have watched them happily or jumped into the middle of their cuddle pile if I wanted to. But right then, I wanted to check on a certain tiger.

Arjun remained silent and detached. He stood in the middle of the living room like he no longer knew what to do. He still wore the pants he had stolen from a human and Lhozen's dried blood on his neck and chest.

"Hey," I said, running my hand along his arm as I approached him carefully. "You okay?"

His arm wrapped around my shoulders, pulling me into his side as that ocean-colored gaze lowered to mine.

"I was just wondering what airline we should fly home on. It's been so long since I flew first class, I forgot which one has the best tea."

"What?" I blinked.

He chuckled, kissing my hairline. "I'm ready to get the fuck out of dodge, dove. As soon as those two can shift, I want to go home and I want to be bloody comfortable on the way there."

"Me too," I admitted. "I wonder if everything went okay with Connor. God, I'm dying to see my siblings again. But," I chewed my lip, blushing. "I've never been on a plane before."

"Ah, yes. I should've known." He squeezed my shoulder affectionately. "First class is going to ruin you, then. You'll never go back to economy seating."

"What's that?" I purposely widened my eyes as big as they could go. "Has Hell frozen over? I just told you something I've never done, and you didn't give me shit for it."

"Because I'm not that thick to take the piss out of a girl when I'm trying to figure out how to get in bed with her."

Now my eyes were wide out of genuine surprise. "You... what?"

"I'm rubbish at this whole seduction thing," he muttered, looking away from me. "I've never really done it before. I'm not brash and outspoken like Connor, silver-tongued like Raz, or cool and aloof like Hunter."

"No, you're not any of them." I brought a hand up to his cheek to make him look at me again. "You're Arjun. You faced your worst fear and taught me everything I knew to bring down evil today. We never, in a million years, could have pulled this off without you." My heart slammed into my throat, but I wouldn't let the rest of my words go unspoken.

"And I love you."

He sucked in a sharp breath as he turned to me, holding my shoulders with both hands.

"Mel—" I raised a hand to cut him off.

"I know you're not into the whole sharing thing and I get that. I don't want to make anything weird for you so I—"

He cut me off with a kiss, hard and possessive, that made me weak in the knees. His tongue forced its way past my lips in a way that felt just as intimate as sex. He didn't kiss or love freely, so my head was completely spinning as I came up for air.

"I told you, you are my mate," he said gruffly. "So what if you're the others' mate, too? You're still mine." His hand released its firm grip on my shoulder and moved up to caress my neck. "And I'm yours, dove. All of me is yours."

"You mean that?" I asked. "But you were so against it before—"

"Because I'm a fool," he muttered, running a thumb across my cheek. "The human side of me is, anyway. My tiger knew all along. Since I first heard your voice in my head. You saved me, my love. Not just from captivity, not just from my fear, but from dying a lonely old man because I was too stubborn to see what was right in front of me."

"Arjun..." I breathed his name as I curled my fingers into his skin. His muscles flexed beneath my hands, matching the needy pulse in my core. I wanted him. I wanted to feel alive with him and never take life or freedom for granted again.

Bits of dried blood flaked under my fingers and I couldn't help laughing as I rubbed it off his chest.

"Rule number one of seduction," I teased, "you should be showered and clean before trying to get a girl in bed with you."

"Right," he chuckled, inspecting himself. "You'd think that'd be common sense, yeah?" he said, wiping at the remaining blood on his chest.

"Rule number two," I said, stepping away as I slid my hand into his. "Showers are much more fun with a partner."

A beautiful grin spread across his face as his eyes lit up. "I like where this is going."

He followed me to his room, bypassing Raz and Hunter, who had fallen asleep in each other's arms. My poor boys had to be exhausted. I was too and a hot, relaxing shower sounded amazing, even when I had taken a bath just a few hours ago. Being with Arjun was just a bonus.

It wasn't until I turned on the hot water and we stood in front of each other that I realized I was still wearing the ridiculous red dress.

"Unzip me?" I turned my back to him and lifted my hair. My skin was practically vibrating with anticipating another touch from him. He finally touched me after what felt like thirty seconds, but nowhere near the zipper.

"It looks beautiful on you," he observed, his palm against the nape of my neck. The other hand came around the front to hold my jaw as he rasped into my ear, "but it would look better on the floor."

"Where'd you hear that one?" I laughed at the cheesiness of the line, but my breath quickly turned to gasps and soft moans as he covered my neck and shoulders with kisses. When he finally unzipped the dress and pulled it down, the kisses continued in a slow, sensual trail down my spine.

A question came to me as I turned around, pulling him toward me with the waistband of his pants. "Have you done this before?"

"Have sex?" He looked surprised, then embarrassed. "Yes. Why?"

"You just seem to know what you're doing." I flicked open the button, then unzipped him slowly. "For someone who was raised to take this stuff so seriously."

He chewed his lip, looking away and letting out a breath as if ashamed. "I had a... friend with benefits, you could say. We were both set up in arranged marriages and kind of commiserated over it. We got along and had physical chemistry, but were never in love. We kept it a secret, because of the shame it would bring to our families."

"Arjun." I said his name as I reached into his pants and filled my palm with him, enjoying the change in expression on his face. "You don't have to be ashamed of having a past. I have one too. Even before I met the other guys."

"I know, it's just," he sighed, rolling his eyes upward. "Mum never knew. She would have been so disappointed. I know it's dumb and doesn't really matter, but I still feel guilty that I wasn't the son she could be proud of." He drummed his fingers against the glass wall of the shower, now filling up with steam. "And especially now that I've killed her husband."

I opened the shower door and stepped inside, pulling him after me. His hands slid around my waist as we stood under the stream of water together.

"If she is watching, I'm sure she's proud of you," I said, watching the rivulets wind down the hard contours of his body. "You saved so many lives today. You overcame your fear. Hell, even if she's not, *I'm* proud of you, Arjun."

"Thank you, dove," he murmured, his pupils large as he looked at me. "She would've liked you, I think," he added with a small smile. "If you were Indian and living in England, she might even approve of me marrying you."

"Hah," I scoffed. "Well, I'm not, and I never was." My hands tangled in his hair, enjoying how the thick, dark tresses moved across my palms from the force of the water. "But I'm here. Right now."

"Yes," he agreed. "You are. And you're *mine*."

His next kiss pushed my back against the marble-tiled wall. I swore I heard a feline growl as his mouth devoured mine. Both of us slippery and wet, he kept me pressed to the wall as he slid down my body.

Kneeling in front of me, he kissed my vulva with just as much passion and hunger as my mouth. A moan escaped me as his tongue parted my folds, one hand reaching up to tease my nipple between his fingers.

I had to take a moment and silently thank his old friend with benefits. He *really* knew what he was doing.

Jolts fired through my limbs as his skilled tongue lashed at my clit. With one large hand, he pressed my hip back, preventing me from bucking against his face as much as I would've liked. So I settled for running my fingers through his hair while he ate me like a fine meal.

And as cats tend to do with their meals, he played with me. Tortured me. He took me to the edge of release, panting and trembling, before moving away to kiss my thighs or the crease in my hips.

"You're the worst," I moaned when he denied me once again, his teeth tracing the edge of my hipbone.

"Oh? Do the others give you what you want so easily?" he smirked, thoroughly enjoying my torment.

"Not always," I admitted reluctantly. "I should've known you'd be such a tease."

"Remember this, dove." His fingertips traced across my inner thighs, swirling and moving over the sensitive skin for the sole purpose of making me quiver. "I didn't fall under your spell like the others. You don't have the same power over me as you do them."

He brought his mouth and fingers right up against my pussy. My tender flesh ached for contact, pressure, sensation, anything.

"What do you mean by that?" I asked, fighting to make words through my brain being a jumbled mess.

"It means you can't tame a tiger."

With that, he sealed his mouth over my clit and pressed two fingers inside me at the same time. I gasped at the sudden fullness, the pressure I'd been craving building up faster than I could handle.

My release came explosively. I shook so hard, he had to press me against the wall to stay upright. Even after coming down from the high, my legs wobbled to the point of sinking to sit on the shower floor.

With a chuckle, Arjun shut off the water and wrapped me in a fluffy, luxurious towel. He carried me to the bed and laid me down gently. When he moved to get up, I grabbed his arm and pulled him back, wrapping my legs around his waist to prevent him from leaving.

"What makes you think you can tame *me*, tiger?"

23

MELODY

Arjun's grin was somewhere between shy and wily. The water droplets clinging to his skin defined his already breathtaking physique even more, and I didn't want to waste one second of not seeing him.

"I'm still wet," he said.

"So am I."

I wrapped a hand around his neck to pull him down to me, not caring that he dripped more water onto my bare skin. The towel underneath me would suffice.

His mouth captured mine as he hovered over me, and I caught the light, musky scent of my sex on his face. I let out a little growl of my own and kissed him harder. Despite not being a shifter, something about my own scent on my man felt animalistic and primal. I had marked him. He was mine.

"Maybe you do have a little tiger in you," he murmured, nipping at the column of my throat as he settled between my legs. His muscular thighs pushed mine apart, and his hands ran down the sides of my body like he was just in awe of me.

I explored him the same way, closing my eyes to relish in the feeling of what his mouth was doing to me. My fingers traced the ridges of his chest and abs like my eyes had done so many times before. I felt where his skin texture changed from the burn scars and had the overwhelming urge to kiss them.

"Roll over," I told him, tapping his arm.

"Why?" His voice was muffled in the crook of my neck as he planted lazy kisses there.

"Because I want to be on top."

"Mm. I'm quite comfortable here, though."

"Really, Arjun?" I sighed, raking my nails up his back. "Is this how it's gonna be every time?"

"Hmm, scratch me again like that and I might reconsider."

Digging in harder this time, I ran my hands slower up that wide, broad landscape of muscle and skin. His response was absolutely erotic, arching under my touch and releasing the hottest sounds, something between a growl and a moan. Jesus, I couldn't get enough of this man. Even if he was infuriating sometimes.

"Fuck me," he groaned, shuddering deliciously. "I should call you kitten instead of dove."

I forgot all about fighting him to get on top, because he started rolling forward, pressing his solid cock against my flesh that was still so sensitive from his teasing earlier. He slid against me a few times without penetration. Again with the torture.

His shaft rested, hot and heavy, on my clit, slowly moving back and forth. He watched me silently, hovering above me as he worked my body into a frenzy with just the slightest movement.

"Enjoying yourself?" I huffed, frustrated and vulnerable under the intensity of his gaze. My thighs squeezed around his hips. My hands grabbed the sheets, his forearms, anything they could. My pussy closed around nothing. And yet, he watched me unravel while practically being as still as a statue.

"Yes," he answered softly. "I could watch the woman I love writhe in pleasure for days. I've never seen anything so beautiful."

Those words made me pause and stare up at him. He returned my stare with a kiss that pressed me down into the pillows, then he pressed forward into me.

The sudden fullness of him forced me to break the kiss with a gasp. That upward curve I saw in the cell was now stroking my inner walls in ways I didn't know could feel so good. My moan echoed around the room as I clung to him, digging my nails into his back again.

His growls were soft, but intense, right next to my ear as his thrusts steadily deepened. To hear his desire without words, that primal expression of pleasure rumbling deep in his chest, was hotter than any dirty talk. It made my legs quiver again, my toes curling into his calf muscles as he filled me to the brim.

"Jesus, Mel," he rasped, pausing while fully seated inside me. Again, he watched in fascination as I shook and convulsed around him. This time I saw his jaw clench against losing his precious control. His dick felt like a hot iron inside me, flexing with the effort to hold back his own release. It made that delicious curve press against me harder and extend my pleasure.

"God, stop that," I laughed. "I can't catch a breath."

"Neither can I," he mused, skimming a palm up the side of my ribcage. He cupped my breast briefly before moving on, caressing my neck and looking at me like I was some kind of wonder of the world. "You're absolutely breathtaking."

Heat rushed through me from head to toe, and it had nothing to with sex. "Aww, I like you when you're sweet." Damn, why were compliments hard for me? Especially from him. Ever since I met him, I wished he would stop fucking around and just say what he meant. Now, after falling for him, hearing words like that were almost overwhelming.

"And you love me every other time?" he teased, nipping my earlobe. "Especially when I'm an arse?"

"Oh, especially then," I groaned.

He slid his arms between my back and the bed, bringing my chest to his with a warm, passionate kiss. In the next moment, we went rolling across the mattress until I was straddling him.

"You wanted to be on top?" he grinned, smugly placing his hands behind his head.

"That doesn't mean I do all the work, tiger," I retorted.

He was still seated inside me and I began a gentle rolling of my hips, enjoying the view from where I sat. His eyes were half-closed and his teeth dug into his bottom lip as I rode him. His biceps bulged from the placement of his arms behind his head and I skimmed my hands down those hard surfaces. Exploring him like he had done me, I smoothed my palms over his chest, pressing into them as I raised and lowered myself on his thick shaft.

When I found that scar tissue along his ribs, I lowered

my mouth to kiss him there. Grazing my lips and tongue across the ridges of his abdomen, I kissed the one on his opposite side.

"Why are you doing that?" His tone was curious, not accusatory.

I braced my forearms on his chest, still riding him at a slow, leisurely pace. "Because I like your body and I want to kiss it?"

"But why my scars?" He brought his arms down to push hair back from my face and caress my neck and back. His blue-green eyes were dark, dilated with lust.

"I don't know," I admitted. "They'll always be a part of you, a reminder of what you went through. It's a painful memory for you but maybe if I kiss them, the memories will hurt a little less."

A breath hitched in his chest as he cupped my face. "Gods, I love you, Mel. What did I ever do to deserve you in my life?"

Our mouths came together in a crash of passion and need. His hands went to my hips, supporting me as he thrust upward. My whole body surged with the pleasure of each impact of him into me. I couldn't control myself and neither could he.

I could only feel, take, and give. I felt him in my fingertips and toes with each hard inch he gave me. When I heard his growls, felt his fingers digging into my flesh, tasted the sweat on his skin, I wanted to give him more. More pleasure, more of me. My brave, beautiful tiger deserved nothing less.

At some point we rolled over again, and he held nothing back, pounding into me and filling me with a delicious ache that I couldn't get enough of. We didn't speak aside from groaning, kisses, and gasps. This was raw and primal, but still so human.

This wasn't a meaningless fuck to further our species, we were lovers. We faced death today. We faced losing each other before we had a chance to begin.

I couldn't speak for Arjun, but I would look back on this every time we came together as one again. I'd kiss him with everything in me and sink into bliss every time he sank into me. I'd kiss his scars and remember how close I came to losing him. And no matter how much he pissed me off, I'd never take my tiger for granted.

His thumb pressed to my clit the moment I started quivering again, and his mouth swallowed my moan. My release came like a tidal wave crashing and he followed, filling me with warmth as he roared into the pillow next to my head.

His heart hammered against mine, his chest a heavy weight on top of me, but I loved the safety and solidness of him. My hands remained wrapped around his back, my thighs attached to his hips.

We stayed like that, kissing and intertwined long after we came down from our highs, as if to make up for all the times we wanted to before, but didn't.

24

CONNOR

"I need to go back."

Miriam, Colt, and Gabe all stared at me, dumbfounded across the table.

"You can't," Miriam said, her voice wavering with concern. "It's too dangerous, Connor. I've seen—"

"Exactly *why* I need to go back," I interrupted her. "I can't just sit around with my thumb up my ass while Mel and the guys are risking their lives. It's been three days. I'm going fuckin' nuts."

"Connor, you're not a shaman or a shifter," she protested, her voice pleading. "You'll be walking into that situation completely unprepared. Do you even know how to get into the compound?"

"I'll figure it out," I said, rising from the table. "I'll go to the hotel first, see who's there and get updates."

"And if no one's there?" The inquiry came from Gabe. "What'll you do then?"

"Why, you volunteering to come with me, Wolf Boy? You gonna help me out by following their scent trail? No?

Then don't fuckin' worry about it. Keep staying all tucked in and cozy in *my* house while I'm out checking on *your* brother."

"It's a valid question, Connor," Colt said, watching me cautiously. "It's not wise to go back there alone with no plan. You have no idea what you're up against."

I kind of do, actually—Arjun's stepfather. The whole thing threw me for such a loop, I couldn't bring myself to tell Miriam, Lhozen's former apprentice. If he was as bad as Arjun said, who knew how far his illusions extended? I couldn't get her involved while the others were dealing with him.

"And what about the four other kids you brought home?" Gabe wouldn't let up. "You're just gonna up and leave them in our care?"

"Jeanie's not a kid. She's been taking care of them since she was, though," I shot back, fighting the urge to punch him in his face. "She's got it handled. They don't need a babysitter."

Finished with the conversation, I hurried out to start the RV. Damn, in times like these, I really needed a smaller vehicle. Now that we had money coming, I could actually think about that stuff. Not that I planned to drive across state lines to rescue my woman with any regularity.

Once the engine roared to life, I propped my prosthetic feet on the dashboard and double checked to make sure everything was secure. I went back to Dr. Selow yesterday, and he made a few minor adjustments. Now the prototypes felt perfect. For a moment at the breakfast table, I had completely forgotten that I didn't have my own legs anymore.

With Mel's gorgeous face in my mind, I tapped my

shirt pocket to ensure the document I got from the doctor was still there. I couldn't wait to see her face when I showed it to her.

Because I *would* see her again. Despite the heart-crushing, shitty feeling that something had gone terribly wrong, I knew my girl wouldn't go down without a fight. And she had a lot of fight in her.

After letting the engine run for a few minutes, I brought my feet down, checked my mirrors, and started driving onto the gravel path.

I had just reached the edge of the property line, where the gravel road became paved again as it wound around the pristine FDR building when I saw them.

Four figures walked alongside each other through the FDR Center grounds. Two tall men, one starkly pale and the other with medium brown skin. Between them, a man with short, dark hair had a tattooed arm over the shoulders of a woman.

My woman.

I'd recognize that raven black hair, doe eyes, and creamy skin from a mile away. My mouth dropped open and I don't know how I didn't have a heart attack right then. They were home, and they were okay.

Thankfully, my brain worked enough to hit the brakes and put the RV in park before stumbling out the door like a drunken sailor.

"Mel?" I hollered as my legs carried me to them, blinking rapidly and rubbing my eyes to make sure it wasn't an illusion. "Babe? Guys, is that you?"

"Going on a camping trip, Con?" Raz joked. He released his arm around Mel's shoulders as she leaped forward, clasping her hands tightly around my neck and her legs around my waist.

"Thank God. Thank fucking God," was all I could utter at feeling her warmth and love wrapped around me.

"Jeanie?" she asked me, eyes wide. "The kids? Are they...?"

"They're all here, babe. Safe and sound," I assured her, taking in her smile, her eyes, and her heart beating against mine. It felt like she'd been away for months instead of mere days. "Fuck, I missed you so much."

"I missed you, too." Her lips found mine and nothing in my life ever tasted sweeter. I wanted to drink her in until my last breath.

Her legs eventually slid down to the ground and our lips parted, though her head stayed firmly attached to my chest. I had no intention of untangling our physical contact today. Maybe not even tomorrow.

"Fellas," I said, holding my arms out to the guys. "It's good to see y'all too. I take it you have a hell of a story for me."

"Like you wouldn't believe, mate," Arjun muttered, clapping his arm around me in a bro hug. I noticed how he touched Mel's waist too and looked at her adoringly. A world of difference from the sneaky looks and pretending to ignore her from before.

Ah, so that finally happened. I lifted an eyebrow at her and she confirmed it with a small nod, a grin threatening to spread across her face.

"Did the pups behave?" Hunter asked when he came in for his hug.

"No," I laughed. "But it's okay. They shifted right in front of Mel's siblings before we had a chance to explain anything. We had an interesting discussion but everything worked out."

"Really?" Mel's brow knitted worriedly. "Jeanie is so protective of the kids. I figured it would be weeks before she warmed up to the idea."

"That might have been ideal, but not practical, with two rambunctious pups running around," I winked at Hunter, who rolled his eyes.

"I'm gonna kill them," he groaned.

"No need. Jeanie had her reservations, but after that talk, she's really warmed up to the shifters. And the kids? They were running around and playing with the pups immediately. It was like they didn't even care. They were so excited just to have new friends to play with."

"Aww, good! They've really needed that." Mel pressed her face into my chest and squeezed around my waist. "They need friends and a real family. A normal life."

"Same with the pups," Hunter agreed, kissing the top of her head. "Having friends, especially."

"Ain't nothing normal about this family," I chuckled, turning around to head back to the RV. "But that's what so great about it."

"Have fun turning that bitch around," Raz laughed. Fucking dragon. I missed him, too.

"Kiss my ass, man. I'll have you know I do beautiful thirteen-point turns in this thing. Babe?" I squeezed Mel into my side. "Ride with me?"

"Sure," she laughed. "All the way back to the house —ahhh!"

I picked her up and threw her over my shoulder caveman style as her screaming-laugh rang out across the landscape. The RV door slammed behind us and I didn't waste any time. I threw her down on that tiny mattress where we made so many memories, and kissed my woman with everything in me.

"God, I missed you so much," I murmured against her skin, kissing every square inch I came across. "I was heading back to Florida because I couldn't stand not knowing if you were okay."

"We had good timing then," she breathed, sliding her legs up around my waist.

I lowered my forehead to hers, watching her face carefully try to hide her expressions. "How crazy was it?"

"Just as Arjun said," she sighed. "Like you wouldn't believe. I don't even know where to start."

"So you and him." I kissed her neck, breathing her in. "How long did it take for that to happen?"

"Well," she laughed lightly. "We got captured, and it technically didn't happen until after we got out."

"Captured? You?"

"All of us." She smoothed her hands up my chest and pushed gently. "We'll tell you everything, but let me up. I want to see my sister."

"Fine," I groaned, pressing her down into the mattress with another hard kiss before releasing her. She joined me in the passenger seat a second later, face flushed and lips swollen. Just how I liked her.

The RV barely got rolling on the gravel path when two blurs raced past us like a pair of bullets toward the house.

"The fuck—"

"It's Arjun and Hunter," Mel laughed. "They shifted and looks like they're racing. Shifters, always competing against each other."

"Fair enough, but where's Raz?"

Tap-tap-tap.

A black claw surrounded by obsidian scales clicked against my driver's side window. Grey eyes and a toothy grin greeted me in my peripheral vision.

"Looks like he gave the others a head start," Mel observed. She leaned over and blew a kiss at the dragon flying alongside us. He responded by licking my window.

"I swear to God, Raz," I yelled, rolling down the window just a crack. "If you make me run over one of these potholes, you're buying me a new car."

He let out a series of grunts that sounded like cackling laughter before flying away, easily beating the running shifters on the ground.

"Oh my God." Mel covered her mouth, blinking away tears as we pulled up to the house. Jeanie stood on the porch with Riley on her hip, the two of them looking skyward and pointing at the dragon flying overhead.

"It's okay, babe." I reached over and squeezed her knee. "She knows about Raz, too. Seriously, she's taken to everything really well. So have the little ones."

"I know, it's just..." she paused to wipe her eyes, then jumped out of her seat, and went running up to the porch the moment the RV stopped. "Jeaniiiieee!"

Not wanting to intrude on them, I watched through the windshield as the girls hugged each other, both of them crying. Bella and Joey, who'd been playing with the pups, screamed Mel's name as they ran to the porch.

Even I had to wipe a tear as I saw them all together. The relief and joy was clear in their tear-streaked faces, how tightly they held each other, and how they laughed uncontrollably with joy.

This was all that Mel had wanted from the beginning.

A safe, loving home for her family. She just happened to take a few detours and met four handsome knuckleheads along the way.

But I had a few more surprises for her and waited until she and her siblings were done hugging.

"Short trip, huh?" Gabe cracked at me as I exited the RV.

"Uh, yeah." I couldn't bring myself to still be pissed at him. Not after witnessing a moment like that.

"Look, sorry about before," he muttered. "I'm glad she's back, and that everyone's okay."

I lifted my chin in surprise. Maybe there was more to the young wolf than being an immature dick. "Thanks, man. I appreciate it."

"Miriam and Colt and I'll be heading home soon," he added, shoving his hands in his pockets. "We'll let y'all have some family time."

"Thanks," I said again. "See you around, Gabe."

"See ya, Connor."

Mel, Jeanie, and the younger ones were making a racket in the kitchen by the time I headed inside.

"We wanna make a cake!" Joey declared.

"Oh, but we need cake-making stuff," Mel answered, lifting her gaze to me and playfully mouthing, *help me.*

I curled my finger at her to beckon her closer, drawing her into the empty theater room.

"Told you they were well-adjusted."

"I'm so relieved," she sighed. "I was worried about how they'd react to... everything."

"Shifters, four boyfriends." I lifted my hands as if weighing both options. "There's probably weirder shit out there."

"Connor." Her smile fell. "How long will we be able to stay here? I know Dr. Selow said as long as you're using their services but with four more people now——"

"I'm so glad you asked, babe." I grinned, fishing the document out of my shirt pocket and waving the papers in front of her face.

"What's that?"

"The deed to the house," I told her. "Dr. Selow gifted it to us. It's ours outright."

"He...what?!" She snatched the papers from me and scanned over them. "How?"

"I'm afraid I'll have to retire from carnival work, babe," I said apologetically. "It won't be feasible with my new job."

Her eyes lifted from the papers slowly, so big and wide I could see myself in them. "What new job?"

"I'm going to be a mentor for the FDR Center," I told her. "They need people to help vets transition to civilian life while taking their disabilities into account. I figure I managed mine pretty well with your help, so..."

"Connor." Mel clasped her hands around my neck. "That's amazing! I'm so proud of you."

"I couldn't have done it without you, babe." I pulled her tight against my chest, loving how perfectly she fit against me. "Fuck, I wouldn't even be standing here if it wasn't for you."

"Neither would I," she whispered. "If it wasn't for you."

I lifted her up as we kissed, spinning her in a circle until she threatened to puke on me.

"Fine. Now get back in the kitchen and make that cake," I said with a slap to her ass when I set her down.

"Jesus, Connor," she groaned, but couldn't fully hide her smile as she rejoined her siblings.

"Oh, what are we making now?" Arjun asked, striding into the house and sliding a hand around her waist. She leaned into him and it filled my heart with joy. About damn time they set aside their differences and realize how good they were for each other.

"A cake!" Riley exclaimed, holding up a wooden spoon.

"Hey, do you turn into a wolf too?" Bella asked him.

"No, young lady. Even better." He stretched a hand out toward her. "I'm a tiger."

His arm grew stripes, fur, and claws right before everyone's eyes.

"Holy shit!" Jeanie cried.

But all the kids just said, "Whoooah!" and reached out to touch him with curious, gentle fingers. Mel beamed brighter than the sun as she watched them.

I couldn't wait to see her like that every day. Not worried or concerned constantly. Of course, she'd still have those days, and I'd be there for her in any way that she needed. But I knew from that point on, as long as her family was safe and she had us to love her, she'd find it so much easier to smile.

EPILOGUE
MELODY

I woke up needing to piss like a racehorse.

I was alone in bed and sunlight filled the bedroom, meaning I had slept in. And goddamn, did it feel good to sleep in my own bed again.

My feet hit the floor, and I almost made it to the bathroom before doubling back to grab the pregnancy test on the nightstand. Connor did not forget after we came home, and apparently did a bunch of research while we were in Florida. He insisted I take the test first thing in the morning because of the higher concentration of pregnancy hormones or whatever.

I just knew he'd be crabby if I forgot, because then he'd have to wait another whole day to find out.

After doing my business in the bathroom, I busied myself with picking up clothes from the bedroom floor and other random little tidying things while I waited for the results to show on the stick. My stomach did flips as I watched the clock on the nightstand once all the clothes were picked up. Three minutes might as well had been three hours.

Finally, I returned to the bathroom and picked up the stick from where I left it on the counter. I looked at the results, then at myself in the mirror.

I could barely breathe. *I need to tell Connor. No, everyone!*

"Babe?" I called down the stairs, but no answer. Only my voice echoed off the ceiling and walls. Not even the kids were making a racket downstairs, which was especially weird.

"Connor?" I made my way down the stairs, clutching the test tightly in my hand.

An empty house greeted me. Not a soul was in sight.

"Jeanie?" I called. "Where the hell is everybody?"

A flash of movement in the backyard caught my eye. I saw my four guys standing together in a row, the pups and the kids fidgeting and squirming off to the side while Jeanie talked to them.

Confused, I opened the sliding glass door and stepped out onto the patio.

"What are you guys doing?"

"*Steluţa*, come here," Raz smirked mischievously. "We want to ask you something."

I shoved the pregnancy test in my pocket as I walked out onto the lawn, narrow-eyed and suspicious. "What are you guys up to?"

My heart stopped when they all dropped to one knee.

"Melody," Connor began. "You saved me from poverty, a life of pain, and from myself. You pushed me to be the man you knew I could be, and I will never stop loving you for that."

"It goes without saying that you saved my life," Hunter

said. "And for as long as we've known each other, you've been the most patient and kind person I've ever met, human or shifter. You showed me family isn't dictated by blood or species and I will always love you for that."

"You trusted me," Raz said next. "When I know it wasn't easy for you to do so. When my life felt meaningless and dark, you, my *steluţa*, showed me the light of your love. I want to spend the rest of my life proving that I'm worthy of your trust because I love you." He turned to Hunter, pressing a kiss to his cheek. "And you."

If my heart wasn't already overflowing, seeing that display of affection between them would have done it for me. I had to admit it softened the anticipation of turning to the beautiful tiger shifter with the ocean-colored eyes and waited for him to speak.

Like when we made love, he did nothing, but look at me for a long moment, saying nothing.

"There are no words," he said with a small shake of his head, never removing his gaze from me. "I could be cheeky or romantic, but none of it would do justice to how I feel about you. Yes, you saved my life. Yes, you helped me face my worst fear. Yes, you gave me the courage to confront the hidden evil I grew up with, but," he paused, "it's not enough just to tell you. I want to spend every minute of every day showing you how much I love you." He broke eye contact with me for the first time, looking at the three men kneeling next to him. "So on that note, we wanted to ask you..."

"Will you marry us?" the four of them said in unison.

"Yes!" I cried. "Of course, I will. Jesus Christ, I wanted to say that a whole five minutes ago!"

"That's what you get when you love four men, *steluţa*,"

Raz laughed, rising to his feet. "We all wanted to say our piece."

They all stood and gathered around me for hugs and kisses, but I couldn't wait to tell them my news any longer.

"I'm pregnant!" I yelled, raising the pregnancy test aloft like a wand.

"What?!" Jeanie shrieked, who had been filming the whole proposal on Connor's phone. "You're having a baby?!"

"Don't worry, Jean," I laughed joyously as my men smothered me in kisses. Someone snatched the test from my hand and they all clamored at each other to see it. "All four of these baby daddies ain't going nowhere."

"Why would we?" Connor voiced huskily, tears glittered in his eyes. "You're our bride. The love of all our lives. So perfect for us in different ways." His hand smoothed over my belly. I laced my fingers with his, soaking up his strength, his protection, his love.

My Marine, my first love, and the father of my child, pressed his lips to my forehead, murmuring gently over my skin, "And this baby will show humans how to love shifters as you have."

THE END...ish

Dear reader,

You are cordially invited to the wedding of Melody, Connor, Hunter, Razvan, and Arjun. Find your invitation, and many more fun extras, in the extended epilogue, ***Backstage at the Freak Show. Available now!***

ACKNOWLEDGMENTS

Jesus tap-dancing Christ! The end of another adventure...

The Harem of Freaks series would not have been possible without my PA, Danielle, Mel and Connor's first fan! I also need to extend my heartfelt thank yous to my beta readers, Sara and Janet for all of your wonderful feedback. Janet, thank you especially for helping me keep Arjun an authentic Englishman!

The amazing Brandy Slaven deserves a massive shoutout for shouting about my Freaks from the rooftops to anyone who would listen. Raz adores his #1 fan!

And I must acknowledge all of Raz's other #1 fans: you, the readers. Thank you for your messages, reviews, reads, and re-reads. It means the world to me to hear how much you relate to Mel or Connor, or any of the others. These Freaks did some magic tricks on our hearts, didn't they? Thank you all so much for loving them as much as I have!

xoxo,
    Crystal

NEWSLETTER & READER GROUP

Never miss a book release, plus get three *free* short stories when you sign up for my newsletter!

Grab your freebies at:
crystalashbooks.com/freebies

You can also join my reader group on Facebook to get updates and hang out with fellow readers.

Join Crystal's Coven at:
facebook.com/groups/crystalscoven

ALSO BY CRYSTAL ASH

Say Your Prayers

<u>Shifted Mates Trilogy</u>

<u>Unholy Trinity: The Complete Series</u>

<u>Harem of Freaks series</u>

Steel Demons MC

Lawless

Powerless

Fearless

Painless

Helpless

Heartless

Senseless

Ruthless

Merciless

For a complete list of books by Crystal Ash, visit her Amazon page.